Published by Pinky Dior

Publisher's Note:
This is a work of fiction. Any names of historical events, real people, living and dead, or the locales are intended only to give the fiction a setting in historic reality. Other names, characters, places, businesses, and incidents are either the product of the author's imagination or are used fictitiously, and their resemblance, if any, to real life counterparts is entirely coincidental.

The Beginning

Meghan

Meghan was distressed behind her boyfriend Ralph's constant infidelity issues. She had enough. She loved him unconditionally and did anything he wanted, but him cheating on her had repelled her from his affection. She had never caught him having sex with another woman, but there was a lot of evidence that exposed his unfaithfulness.

Meghan had been in a relationship with Ralph since she was fourteen years old. She had given him her most precious prized possession: her virginity. When she was young, she had vowed never to have sex with any man until she man until she got married. Nevertheless, she went against her vow when she fell in love with Ralph the first day she laid eyes on him. Here she was eighteen years old and it still felt like she was dealing with the same adolescent she had met several years ago.

They were making love when he called her another female's name. "Nikki" was the name he seductively called out while moaning, "This is the last time!"

Meghan cocked her head back but continued riding him with a sour look on her face. She couldn't believe he had the audacity to call her another female's name, especially during sex. Her blood was boiling inside and it felt like hot lava about to erupt from a volcano. Meghan didn't stop having sex with him; she mustered up a moan to boost his ego. Within seconds, she fabricated a fake orgasm.

Before she could get off of him, he gripped her body tightly and exploded inside of her. Quickly, she got off top of him and lay down on the bed, turning her back towards him.

"What's wrong, baby?" Ralph said in between heavy breaths.

"Nothing," Meghan lied. She wiped away a warm tear that barely made it past her cheekbone.

Ralph breathed heavily as he basked in the bed in his master bedroom for several seconds before getting up. Meghan could hear his heavy feet walking across the tiled floors as he made his way towards the bathroom. Meghan scrunched up her face when her boyfriend started peeing in the toilet and didn't bother closing the door.

"Fucking pig!" she mumbled. She was just in disbelief over what had just happened while they were having sex. Lately she thought they were on good terms - until it was brought to her attention that Ralph was cheating on her - but she didn't want to believe the rumors. The evidence she had of him cheating and now someone telling her personally caused her to think it had to have some truth to it. If you called your girl another female's name during sex, that meant you were fucking someone else. Meghan didn't take that lightly, and this was the final straw.

Ralph emerged from the bathroom, slipped into the bed, and got under the sheets with Meghan. He wrapped his arms around her waist, kissed her, and said, "I love you" as if he hadn't just called her another female's name.

Meghan didn't even both saying the three-letter word back. She just pretended to be asleep.

Meghan stared into the darkness of the room, waiting for Ralph to fall asleep. She knew he was in a deep sleep when he started snoring loudly. Meghan grabbed his hand, which was wrapped around her waist, and gradually picked up his arm as she wiggled her body closer to the edge of the bed. Once out of the bed, she gently placed his hand back down on the bed, hoping he didn't wake up. She looked back and noticed he was still in a deep sleep. She tiptoed across the tiled floor, and when it creaked, she immediately stopped in her tracks. Immediately her face tightened up and she looked back over her shoulders. Ralph was tossing around in the bed. Meghan thought he would feel her absence, but seconds later, he went back to snoring.

Meghan sighed in relief as she made it safe and sound to the other side of the room. She got dressed quickly, trying to make as little noise as possible. She snatched up her fake Gucci purse and walked several feet across the room to Ralph's safe. Placing a long strand of hair behind her ear, she bent down and started to punch in the numbers to Ralph's safe. She was the only one who knew the code because he knew she would never steal from him. That's why she was the only person to have it. He trusted her more than he trusted himself.

Once the safe cracked open, Meghan unzipped her purse and removed the several stacks of money from the safe, stuffing them into her bag. As she put the money in her book bag, every few seconds she was looking over her shoulders to make sure he didn't wake up as she robbed him completely blind. There was diamond jewelry and other accessories in the safe as well that she originally wasn't going to touch, but she changed her mind. *Ahh, what the heck?* Meghan shrugged her shoulders as she cleaned up the safe, stuffing everything into her purse, leaving nothing behind.

Meghan slowly got up from the floor, tossing her purse over her shoulder as she tiptoed out of Ralph's bedroom. She thanked God that he lived by himself; otherwise, she probably would have gotten caught. As soon as she reached the end of the hallway and opened up the front door, it made a loud squeaky noise.

"Meghan?" Ralph called out.

Shit! That's when she opened up the door and ran for her life. She knew that if she stayed any longer, he would eventually find out about his safe. He was so overprotective of his safe that he checked it every time he woke up and sometimes before he went to sleep.

Meghan was out of breath as Ralph yelled after her. He must have checked his safe right away and noticed that she had emptied it. Meghan left nothing but a pawn slip inside for a piece of jewelry. Meghan was halfway down the street when she turned back and noticed Ralph exiting the house butt naked. She laughed as she ran all the way down the block. He eventually stopped chasing her once he noticed everyone was staring at him. She made it as far away from his apartment as she could. She knew she couldn't afford to be seen by any of Ralph's friends or the people he knew. She knew for a fact he probably had his boys on the lookout for her.

Meghan caught a Gypsy cab and headed home. She didn't think it was a good idea, but she figured that Ralph wouldn't assume she would go home right away, especially after robbing him and given the fact that he knew where she lived. Before exiting the cab, she looked out the window for any signs of Ralph or his car, but she didn't see anything. She almost thought he would have been some type of Superman and awaited her at her front door. She handed the driver a ten dollar bill and exited the cab. She quickly walked down the path to her house, removing the keys from her hoodie. She opened up the door, and her mother was sitting down at the kitchen table.

"You got out of hair school early. I was waiting for you."

"Ma, I'm not a little kid," Meghan informed her mother as she removed her purse strap from her shoulder and set it down on the couch "I got out earlier and I was out and about," Meghan said as she sat down at the kitchen table.

"Just because you're eighteen you think you can do as you please, huh?" Loretta asked as she pulled out a cigarette and placed it in between her index and middle finger. She placed the Newport between her succulent big lips, brought the lighter up to it, and blew the smoke in Meghan's direction.

Meghan hated when her mother smoked around her, and she knew her mother only did that to agitate her sometimes. Meghan waved her hand side to side, diverting the smoke from heading in her direction.

"No, Ma," Meghan said as she sighed dejectedly. "I need to tell you something though."

"Tell me what?" She took a long drag on her Newport and squinted her eyes. "You pregnant or something?"

"Hell no!" Meghan cracked a smile, shaking her head from side to side. "I'm not pregnant."

"Watch your mother!" Loretta gave her daughter the evil eye as she continuously smoked her cigarette.

Meghan nervously bit down on her bottom lip. She knew her mother wouldn't approve of what she was about to say, but she just blurted it out anyway. "I'm moving to Palm Beach."

"You're moving to what, to who?" Loretta asked, being sarcastic. She spoke in between coughs and choking on the cigarette smoke. "No daughter of mine is moving to Palm Beach! Mmm, mmm, child…no!" Loretta shook her head, pursed her lips together, and stood firm about what she said as she jabbed the cigarette on the ashtray.

"I have to," Meghan said as she stared her mom in the eye. "I mean, I wanted to go, I've been saving up money to go, but now I have to go. Ralph is after me."

"Why is Ralph after you?" Loretta became suspicious as her eyebrows arched up.

Before Meghan could respond, there was a boisterous banging on the door that startled them both. Meghan was startled, breathing heavily as she stared at the front door. She ran to the couch, picked up her purse, and rushed back towards the kitchen.

"Tell him I'm not here," Meghan informed her mother as she rushed down the hall. She slipped into the laundry room and stood in the doorway with her heart beating rapidly.

She listened carefully and she could hear her mother opening up the front door. She didn't hear the second door open, so she knew she had left the screen door closed and locked. Meghan eavesdropped on her mother Loretta and Ralph's conversation. She talked to him through the screen door. She was hoping and praying he didn't ask to come in.

"Hi, Ralph."

"Hi, Ms. Loretta. Is Meghan here?"

"Oh no, baby, she isn't here," Loretta lied. "She got out of school early and I ain't seen her since this morning."

"Well, if you see her, can you just call me? I have a surprise for her."

Lying-ass motherfucker! Meghan thought to herself as she rolled her eyes and waited for Ralph to leave. *He probably got an ass whooping for me or he might try to kill me.*

"Okay, baby, I will do that," Loretta said. "Bye-bye now." She closed the door and locked it behind her.

Meghan emerged from the laundry room and headed down the hall, where her mother stood there with her hands on her hips.

"You want to tell me what's really going on?"

"I broke into his safe and took out everything he had, and I have to leave town or he's going to kill me." Meghan let it all out in a few seconds and gulped down hard when she was finished. She knew her mother was going to have a field day with this one.

"Meghan!" Loretta shrieked as she smacked her forehead and shook her head from side to side.

"I know, Ma, I messed up, but he cheated on - "

"I don't want to hear it, Meghan," she said as she continuously shook her head. "You're going to get whatever you stole from him and give it back."

"I'm not."

"You are."

"I'm not!" Megan barked with a stern look. "I'm moving to Palm Beach and no one's going to stop me…including you," she said as she walked towards the front door and placed her hand on the doorknob.

"Meghan, if you leave out that front door, don't you ever come back," Loretta said without any emotion. "You hear me?"

Meghan turned around and told her mother that she loved her and would be in contact with her, but her mother turned her back on her daughter and didn't say it back. Tears formed in Meghan's eyes as she looked at her mother. Her back was turned towards her and her head hung to the side.

"Mama?" Meghan couldn't believe her mother was acting like that. "I love you." The tears that filled up in her eyes streamed down her warm cheeks. She stared at her mother, who wouldn't dare turn to look at her. She didn't even say "I love you" back. Meghan bit down on her lips and held back more tears that were built up. She bobbed her head as she turned the doorknob and exited the house, never looking back.

***

Meghan was waiting for her best friends to meet her at the diner near Mass Avenue. She had been impatiently waiting for them for about an hour and a half. She started to remove her pink Nokia cell phone from her white and pink-hearted sweater to call them again. Simultaneously, Nicolette and Carmen both walked in through the front door of the diner. Meghan smiled as she slid her phone back into her sweater pocket.

"What's up?" Carmen popped her strawberry bubble gum loudly as she walked towards Meghan with her hands in her denim jacket. "What's the emergency?" She slid into the booth and Nicolette did the same.

"Ralph is after me," Meghan whispered.

"Why, what did you do?" Carmen asked with a heavy Spanish accent.

"I found out he was cheating on me," Meghan said. "He called me another girl's name while we was having sex earlier today." She sighed dejectedly as she lifted her head up and fanned her eyes to keep the tears from falling.

"Awww, I'm so sorry," Carmen apologized to her as if she was the guilty party.

"Don't be." Meghan said as she shook her head. "You weren't the one sleeping with my man."

"So why is he after you if he's the one who cheated on you?" Nicolette asked inquisitively, wanting to know why her best friend had paged her using the code 911 for an emergency.

"Because I robbed him for everything," Meghan said as she removed the bag from beside her and plopped it onto the table. She unzipped it, discreetly showing it to the girls, allowing them to get a little peek inside of the bag. Their eyes lit up with dollar signs as they stared into the bag. Meghan had counted up the money she had stolen from Ralph. It was only $20,000 dollars. Meghan assumed Ralph had way more money since he was dealing drugs, but if he did, she thought he would have had it in that same exact stash spot. Meghan quickly closed up the bag and placed it by her side.

"I'm leaving tomorrow afternoon to catch a flight to Palm Beach, so if y'all coming with me, let me know by the morning."

"Did you tell your mother?" Carmen asked.

"Yeah, and she doesn't approve of me going," Meghan said, shrugging her shoulders without a care in the world. "But I would be crazy to stay and become one of Ralph's next victims." She pursed her lips together, shaking her head from side to side, letting her friends know that staying here was out of the question. Meghan would be a fool to stick around knowing what her boyfriend was capable of. Although he was mainly a drug dealer, she had watched as he beat a man to death one day just for owing him a hundred dollars. She ran her fingers through her light brown hair and twisted it around her index finger.

"What about us finishing cosmetology school and then going?" Carmen asked curiously. She was currently in cosmetology school along with Meghan. Meghan's passion was for hair, and Carmen's was doing makeup.

"I'll finish it out there, and y'all can finish up school too," Meghan said, making it sound good. "We should all go so we can meet us some rich men and live the lavish life."

Both Nicolette and Carmen busted out laughing hysterically, as if they were watching a comedian on TV.

"What's so funny?" Meghan asked as she slowly unraveled her hair from her finger, waiting for a response.

"You really think that if you just up and leave and move to Palm Beach, you're going to find a rich man just like that?" Nicolette said in between laughs.

"You never know; it could be done," Meghan said, defending her words. "The only way you will know is if you go."

"I know I said I would move with y'all to Palm Beach, but I just can't leave my mother like that."

"I mean, I can't tell you what to do, Nicolette, but I'm leaving and that's that." Meghan got up, grabbed her purse, and tossed it over her right shoulder. "If y'all are serious about moving to Palm Beach with me, y'all will be at the airport at 10:00 a.m. sharp." She smiled as she removed herself from the booth and exited the diner. She hoped that her best friends would join her to move to Palm Beach to start a new life.

Nicolette

As soon as Nicolette left the diner, she went straight home. She told Carmen she would call her later. As she walked home, she gave Meghan's idea of moving to Palm Beach some thought. They had always talked about moving out of state, moving specifically to Palm Beach. They were all tired of living in the hood and they yearned for a better life. She just figured they wouldn't be moving so soon. They were supposed to finish school first.

Nicolette knew that moving to Palm Beach would be hard. Her mother was very sick and she had been diagnosed with cancer, but several months ago the doctors declared that it was gone. She didn't even know she had cancer until she went to the doctor and they informed her of it several years ago. Nicolette was very close to her mother April. She knew she just couldn't up and leave like her mother like that. She knew Meghan would be disappointed because she wanted them all to move to Palm Beach and live together.

Nicolette took her key out of her Louis Vuitton purse and slid it into the front door. She saw her Aunt Sarah and her husband Ben on the couch. He had his arms wrapped around her, consoling her. With a baffled facial expression, Nicolette turned around and locked the door behind her. She turned around and walked into the living room.

"What's wrong with her?" Nicolette asked as she stared at her aunt, who looked up at her and broke down into more tears, sobbing uncontrollably.

Ben looked up and a tear slid down his cheek as he opened up his mouth to speak, but no words came out. Nicolette stood with her hand on her hip, waiting for a response. She watched as he removed a single tear with his index finger, wiping it on his pants.

He mustered up his words to speak and finally it came out. "It's your mother."

"What about my mother?" Her voice changed, sadness written across her face. She didn't wait for Ben to answer. She assumed something was terribly wrong with her mother due to her aunt sobbing loudly, as if something terrible had happened.

Nicolette rushed down the corridors and pushed open the door to her mother's bedroom. Her sister Camilla was on her knees, clasping her hands together with their mother's hands between hers. Nicolette rolled her eyes at her sister Camilla. Her sister was half Caucasian and half African American. Nicolette always bumped heads with her because Camilla thought she was the better sister. They shared the same mother but had different fathers. They also didn't live together. Camilla was twenty-five years old, six years older than Nicolette.

Camilla stood 5'6" tall. She had long, thick, light brown hair, freckles decorating her face, and hazel eyes. She was slim but her thighs were thick, her breasts were perky, and her buttocks were nice and firm as if she performed squats every day. Nicolette had to admit, her sister was very beautiful. She looked like she could be a model. She just never got along with her sister.

"What the hell are you doing here?" Nicolette said rudely.

"Mother's dead," Camilla whispered without taking her eyes off her mother.

No matter how much she despised her sister, everything went out the window with that statement. Nicolette rushed to her mother's side and dropped her Louis Vuitton purse to the floor like it had no value.

"No, that can't be possible," Nicolette said with tears in her eyes. She dropped to her knees and stared at her mother. Her eyes were closed and she looked very peaceful. "The doctors said her cancer went away."

"Well, it came back," Camilla stated as she stood up and slid her black purse onto her arm and set the strap on top of her shoulder. "The ambulance is on the way."

Nicolette pulled up a stool next to her mother's bedside and grabbed both of her hands. They were now cold. She sucked in her lips, her eyes submerged with tears. She tried to hold them back, but she couldn't. Tears continuously fell freely from her eyes, like rain did from the sky when it stormed relentlessly.

"I love you, Mother," Nicolette spoke to her as if she could hear her. "I didn't think you would be leaving me so soon. What am I supposed to do now with no mother? I have nobody else. I thought the doctor said your cancer went away? What happened?" Her voice cracked as she spoke. "I know you're going to heaven, Ma. You're in a better place now…I just know it. Just please watch over me. I love you." Nicolette reached over and planted a kiss on her mother's stiff and cold cheek. It felt like she had been dead for hours. "How long has she been like this?"

"I don't know." Camilla shrugged her shoulders nonchalantly. "She called me early this morning, saying she wanted me to take her grocery shopping, and when I got here, I found her just like this," Camilla said as she took one last look at her deceased mother.

Nicolette found that odd because their refrigerator was filled with food and so were their cabinets. "You probably killed her," Nicolette said bitterly.

Camilla walked around the bed and her heels clicked on the wooden floor. Standing in front of Nicolette, "You would say something like that! You're very ignorant with a lack of morals. I don't know where you get that shit from…maybe your drunken daddy." Nicolette got up and smacked her sister across the face. Camilla shook her head and smiled with a sinister laugh.

"Just because you're half black doesn't mean you're better than me. Just because you're half black doesn't make you perfect."

"I never said it does, Nicolette. You're just mad at the fact that your mother got pregnant by a black man with me, but got pregnant by a Caucasian man and had you…oh wait, that's not it. You're just mad because my father practically raised me, bought me anything and everything his little girl wanted. And my daddy wasn't a drunk like yours."

"You sound dumb!" Nicolette barked. "What I'm mad about is how my mother always felt like you were the better child, more beautiful than me. I don't know, that's just how I felt and you proved it. Your father always brought you shit, and my daddy was a fucking drunk who would bring me home a pack of beer and ask me to drink with him," she said with tears forming in her eyes. "You are right," Nicolette agreed with her.

"You think my life was perfect, Nicolette? Huh?" Camilla shrieked. "Mother acted like that when we were around certain people. I won't deny Mother loved me. She truly loved me, but she was scared of what others might think of her, that she slept with a black man. Before you were born, I stayed with our mother until I was five and she handed me off like I was a fucking piece of chicken or something." Camilla gulped down hard, tears brimming from her eyes. "She didn't want me because I was half black. I don't have blue eyes like you do, I don't have blonde, nice, soft silky hair like you do…I don't!" Camilla titled her head to the side.

"So for you to judge me because I'm half African and you're just Caucasian isn't right. Our own mother sent me to live with my father, and she only entertained me on the weekends. You think I didn't want to live with my mother? She was ashamed for sleeping with a black man, so she just sent me away, sweeping me under the rug like a piece of fucking dirt." Camilla sniffled, wiping away the tears from her wet face. She just poured her heart out, and for the first time, Nicolette felt for her.

"I-I'm sorry," Nicolette apologized sympathetically. She hadn't known the entire story.

"No, it's okay, but you need to learn your place," Camilla informed her. "Remember you had a mother and a father, no matter how much of a drunk he was. I only had a father. Mother didn't raise me; my father did, and I commend him for that. I commend him for putting his life on hold, including the woman he loved and the child he brought into this world and didn't take care of like he should have. Now that is a man that I commend," Camilla stated with much pride. "I can't say the same about Mother." Camilla wiped away the rest of her tears. "Excuse me." Camilla held onto her purse strap and walked out of the room, her heels clicking against the wooden floors.

Nicolette sighed dejectedly, running her hands through her unruly long blonde hair. She couldn't believe her mother had done that to her sister. Her mother never told her the truth; she never told her why their sister didn't stay with them. She just made it seem like her sister had a choice to live with her father and that's what she had done. But Nicolette still loved her mother the same no matter what she did to her sister. She was dead now, and she didn't think it was a good idea to blame her and bring up the past. It was too late.

Nicolette kissed her mother one last time on the forehead before exiting her mother's bedroom. She headed into her own bedroom with her head down as she texted her best friend Meghan. *I'll meet you at the airport tomorrow. Looks like I'm heading to Palm Beach after all.* She ended the text with a smiley face, although she wasn't smiling. All Nicolette could do was cry. She grabbed her duffle bag and luggage from her closet. She stuffed as much clothes as she could to take with her to Palm Beach.

There was a light knock on her door. She turned around, wanting to see who it was. Nicolette rolled her eyes at the sight of her sister.

"And where do you think you're going?"

"Palm Beach," Nicolette said as she continued to pack her bags.

"For what?" Camilla questioned, curious to know. She leaned against the doorframe with her arms folded across her breasts.

Nicolette turned around. "Mother's dead. My dad is a fucking drunk, nowhere to be found. What else is there to stay in Boston for?"

"I guess you're right; there's nothing here for you," Camilla said sarcastically with a smile on her face. "You have no mother, no money, no nothing."

"I'm quite sure Mother left me with something." Nicolette stared at her sister as she shook her head and pursed her lips together.

"Mother was broke. She didn't even have an insurance policy that was worth much. She only had a $1,000 life insurance policy."

"That's a lie!" Nicolette shrieked. "Mother told me if anything ever happened to me, she wouldn't leave me without a pot to piss in or without any money or a roof over my head. $1,000? I know that's a lie, Camilla."

"Well…" Camilla licked her lips. "Things happen, Nicolette. I'll take care of everything, and once you arrive in Palm Beach, call me and let me know where you're staying. I will send you the one thousand dollars that's entitled to you."

"I'm curious to know… If half of the inheritance is five hundred dollars, why are you giving me the entire thing? That doesn't make sense." Nicolette was deeply thinking about her sister's motives behind it. Nicolette didn't know why she felt that way, but she knew a scheme when she saw one and she felt as if her sister was scheming her somehow.

"Don't worry about me. I'm all set." She winked at me.

"Whatever." Nicolette shook her head and continued packing.

"Oh yeah, one thing before I go." Camilla cleared her throat. "Mother didn't want to have a funeral, plus she didn't have enough life insurance, for that matter." She sucked her teeth, causing her cheek to jump quickly. "You don't have to worry about coming back. She wanted to be cremated."

"I still want to attend her service. When is it?"

"There's no point in staying. She's not having a service."

"I'll give her one with my money then if that's the case."

"She doesn't have enough money to pay for a service!" Camilla became agitated as Nicolette kept talking about their mother's service.

"You know what's funny?" Nicolette chuckled as she turned around and placed her hand on her hip. "As soon as Mother dies, you come scurrying over here, thinking that you've been in her life all this time, like you deserve something, like you're about to get something," Nicolette assumed. "You seem like you're happy that Mother died. What's up with that?" Nicolette asked inquisitively, honestly wanting to know why.

"I'm not happy Mother is dead, but she's at peace now." Camilla smiled. "I just want her to be buried the way she wanted. She wanted to be cremated and I'm going to make sure I fulfill everything she wanted, down to what she wanted you to have: 1,000 dollars."

"You know what, Camilla? I honestly hate your guts right now." Nicolette's eyes widened in disgust at her sister. There was something about her that wasn't right. Nicolette watched as her sister removed her purse from her shoulders and removed her wallet. She peeled off five crisp one hundred dollar bills and handed them to Nicolette.

"Take this for your plane ticket," Camilla said as she stuck her wallet back in her purse. "Sorry for Mother's loss," Camilla said before exiting the room and disappearing down the hallway.

"Sorry for Mother's loss," Nicolette said, mocking her sister with an absurd look as she stuffed the money into her bra. "Shut up!" Nicolette barked as she zipped up her duffle bag and dropped it to the floor. Nicolette didn't know what her next move would be. She really hoped once she got there, she would meet a rich man like Meghan said, although in her mind she thought it was unlikely that she would meet a rich man so quickly. Nicolette anticipated she would eventually meet someone who could sweep her off her feet and give her the finer things in life. *Palm Beach, here I come!*

Carmen

After meeting up with her besties, Carmen walked home with her purse hanging over her shoulder. Her long hair was tamed into two French-braided ponytails which flowed down both of her shoulders. Carmen was eighteen years old and she attended cosmetology school with Meghan, but not for hair. She loved doing makeup. She wanted to be a famous makeup artist when she got older. She hoped that one day she could open up some type of store to do people's makeup and eventually start her own makeup line.

As soon as Carmen got home, she removed her purse and laid it on her dresser. She kicked off her shoes and lay down on her bed. She removed the picture of Palm Beach from her sweater pocket. She grabbed a nail from another picture as it fell to the floor and placed the picture of Palm Beach on her wall. She stared at the picture for several seconds. She always wondered what it would be like to move to Palm Beach.

Carmen hated living with her mother ever since her new boyfriend Hector had moved in a couple of months ago. Carmen didn't feel comfortable walking around the house in her boy shorts and mini tank tops anymore. It used to be only her and her mother Isabella living there, so at the time she didn't care. But now with a man in the house, she made sure she was always fully clothed, especially with the way he stared at her all of the time.

An unexpected knock on Carmen's door startled her, making her sit up quickly in her full-sized bed. Before she could part her full lips to speak, the door slowly opened, causing a creaking noise. Carmen gulped down hard when she noticed Hector walking into her bedroom.

"What are you doing in my room?" Carmen asked as she placed a piece of hair behind her ear. She had her knees pressed against her chest while her arms were wrapped around them.

Hector didn't say anything. He just closed the door behind him, locked it, and walked over to the bed. Carmen didn't know why he was locking the door, but as soon as he got closer to her and caressed her face, she knew exactly why.

"Don't touch me!" Carmen smacked his hand away and he quickly smacked her across her face.

Carmen was shocked as she held the side of her face and put her hand over her mouth, breathing heavily. Hector slid down his pants and removed them from around his ankles, leaving them on the floor along with his boxers. Carmen eased back on the bed as Hector climbed onto it.

"Please don't do this…please." Tears filled Carmen's eyes as Hector moved in closer. She kept backing up on the bed until she came up against the headboard and couldn't go any further. Carmen's watery eyes moved towards the door, thinking about making a run for it.

"Ah-ah ahhhhh…" Hector cooed as he snatched Carmen's chin so hard you could hear the side of her neck crack in the process. He guided her chin back in his direction, so she could face him. Tears escaped from her hazel eyes and streamed down her cheeks excessively.

"You're mines. I finally got your sexy ass all to myself." Hector smiled, followed by a sinister laugh. Carmen cried some more as he snatched down the skirt she was wearing, leaving all of her other clothes on.

"You don't have to do this, Hector!" Carmen cried as she tried to get him to change his mind.

But he was already on top of her and forcing his hardened shaft inside of her tight vagina. Carmen started screaming out for dear life, but Hector slapped her quickly across her mouth and started humping her harder. Hector's prolonged moans and Carmen's muffled cries were all you could hear throughout her bedroom. She felt like she was being ripped into shreds as his hardened shaft pumped in and out of her dry vagina. Carmen bit his hand and he screamed. Instantly he stopped and looked at his hand.

"You stupid bitch!" he barked as he punched Carmen's face so hard against that she got knocked out.

Several minutes later when she woke back up, Hector was still on top of her, sexing her hard as he fondled her breasts. Carmen was too weak to try and stop or fight against Hector. She just lay there as he enjoyed raping her without a care in the world. Tears blurred her vision again as she stared up at the ceiling, wishing this was all a dream. There was a sudden knock on the door, but it didn't stop Hector from continuing to fuck her hard. He was about to nut, so he kept going even harder as the knocks on the door became more persistent.

The loud banging of the door hitting the cheap walls caused Hector to stop. He looked back and noticed his girlfriend Isabella standing there. He must not have locked the door all the way because her mother had managed to get in. Hector was letting off loads of cum into her daughter as he kept his eyes glued to Isabella. Carmen looked at her mother with a helpless look that read, "Help me", but her mother didn't feel any type of remorse for her daughter. Instead, she was ashamed.

"Carmen, what are you doing?" Isabella walked further into the room. "Why are you fucking my man?" she asked, not sounding surprised.

"Ma, h-he raped me!" Carmen cried as she got off the bed and rushed over to her mother. She hugged her for comfort, only to be pushed away. Carmen fell to the floor, staring at her mother with a baffled facial expression, wondering why she had just pushed her.

"You are a little nasty bitch!" Isabella barked as she raised her finger, pointing it at Carmen. "I always knew you were the type to fuck someone else's man. No wonder the last man left me - because you didn't know how to keep your fucking legs closed!"

Carmen was more hurt by her mother's words than mad. Although Carmen was no angel, she couldn't believe her mother's shady accusations. She could hear her mother talking calmly to Hector, as if he was the one who had gotten raped.

"I want you out."

Carmen looked up from the bloodstained carpet and looked at her mother, who stood with her arms folded across her breasts like a mad Spanish woman.

"I want you out by the morning. I don't care where you go!" Isabella turned around and stormed out of her daughter's bedroom, crying hysterically. Hector turned and looked at Carmen, who was staring back at him. She was breathing hard. She stared at him, intensely, wishing she could kill him right now. Carmen wasn't expecting an apology, but she wasn't expecting the next words she heard from him.

"You got some good pussy." Hector winked and grabbed his limp shaft through his pants and walked out, slamming the door behind him.

Carmen broke out into hysterical cries. She crawled on the floor until she made it to the bathroom. She felt violated.

Carmen looked up in the mirror, noticing the bruise Hector had created on her face. Rolling her eyes, she grabbed the makeup from the cabinet. Tears escaped her pretty hazel eyes and streamed down her red, bruised face. *There's nothing makeup can't cover.* She decorated her face with a good amount of makeup so that no one could tell she had been hit.

Carmen finally made up her mind as she emerged from the bathroom. She grabbed her luggage and started stuffing all of her clothes inside. Carmen knew if she didn't live there with her mother and boyfriend, she'd be better off. She decided she was going to run away with Meghan - and Nicolette, if she decided to go to Palm Beach. She needed a new start.

Meghan

As the airplane slowly began its descent to the ground, Meghan opened her eyes slowly. They fluttered up and down then opened completely. Meghan had never ridden on an airplane before, and she was scared for her life, especially after what had happened on 9/11. She was petrified of going on planes. She had slept for most of the airplane ride. Meghan glanced over at Nicolette, who was staring at a picture of her mother that she held in her hand. She seemed down. Tears filled her eyes, but not one ever escaped.

"What's wrong?" Meghan asked curiously.

"Nothing." Nicolette blinked her eyes quickly as several tears escaped. She sniffled, removing the tears that stained her face with the back of her hand. Nicolette slid her picture back in her purse, got up, grabbed her carry-on bags from over their heads, and exited the plane.

Meghan wondered what was wrong with her. She had never seen her like that before. She could sense that something was wrong with her best friend. She just didn't know what could possibly be wrong.

Shrugging her shoulders, she stood up, retrieving her carry-on. As she emerged from the airplane, her ears popped. Rubbing her ears, she walked through the terminal and went to the area where their luggage would be arriving soon. After the girls got their luggage, they exited the airport and waited for a cab. There were so many people waiting for cabs. They stood there for a good fifteen minutes before one became available to them.

They arrived at the historic Chesterfield Hotel located in Palm Beach, Florida. Meghan, Nicolette, and Carmen hopped out of the taxicab. The cab driver popped the trunk and helped the ladies get their luggage out of the trunk. Meghan tilted her head back and stared at the beautiful exterior of the hotel. After retrieving their luggage, Meghan checked them into the hotel and they made their way up to their rooms. Meghan was in awe as she slid the open the door to their room. This was the most beautiful hotel that they had ever been to. They were staying in the luxurious penthouse suite. The bedrooms were a cream and brown color with a leopard accent. Two queen superior bedrooms with distinct interior were at either end of the room and they each had a separate marble bathroom. The living room was furnished with a desk, chair, a cream sofa, and two sitting chairs.

"Now this is a hotel!" Nicolette said as she touched the drapery on the curtains. "How much did this hotel cost?" she asked inquisitively.

"Don't worry about it," Meghan said, not wanting to tell her how costly the hotel was. "Just know we have to look for jobs or something, because we can't stay here for too long," Meghan said as she stepped inside of one of the bedrooms. It was so gorgeous. She had never seen anything like it before except on TV. She placed her duffle bag on the bed, sliding off her jacket and tossing it on top of her bag.

"I bet this hotel will run you at least two grand a night." Carmen shook her head as she plopped down on the sofa, reclining her feet.

Meghan sat on the comfortable queen-sized bed and fell back onto it. Basking in the warm, comfortable bed made her feel fatigued. She rolled over in the bed and opened up the nightstand drawer, looking for the Yellow Pages. She picked it up and sat up on the bed with her back resting on the fluffy pillows that were situated above the headboard. She scanned through the Yellow Pages, looking for a place to rent a car. They definitely would need a car to get around. She came up on a place. She retrieved the hotel notepad and pen and jotted down the telephone number and address. Meghan got off the bed, emerging from the room holding a piece of paper in her hand and the Yellow Pages in another.

"Where are you going?"

"I'm going to go rent a car. Y'all coming?"

"Nah, I'll stay." Carmen stood up and walked over to Meghan, "We have to start looking for a place to live, right?" Carmen gently removed the Yellow Pages from her hand and pushed Nicolette's legs off the armrest as she sat down next to Nicolette on the couch.

Meghan looked at Nicolette, who rolled her eyes at Carmen. She jumped up to her feet and said, "Nah, I'm staying. I need to get some rest." Nicolette yawned, covering her mouth with her hand. "I'm not feeling to well."

"Alright, I'll be back," Meghan said as she exited the hotel room. She took the elevator down to the lobby and exited the hotel. She stood outside waiting for a taxi to take her to her destination.

***

Rent a Luxury Car was the name of the rental car place Meghan decided to go to. They needed a car to navigate Palm Beach, so Meghan decided to rent a car. She just didn't want to rent any cheap car. She wanted to blend in with the rest of the folks that were driving luxurious cars. Although she only had around twenty thousand dollars, she decided to go out in style. She had never even seen or had that type of money before, but she knew that money went quickly, and the money she stole would only last her a short time. Scanning the lot, Meghan walked around the cars, contemplating which one she wanted.

The lot only had about ten cars, but they were all nice and hard to choose from. There was an all-silver Maybach 57 which caught Meghan's eyes. She walked around the car and she slid her hand over the body of the car, admiring the exterior.

"If you touch the car, you must rent," a deep baritone voice said out of nowhere.

Meghan quickly turned around and noticed a handsome brown-skinned brother in a black suit. Meghan guessed he was in his late twenties. His hair was cut low and he had a little bit of facial hair. As soon as he smiled, it melted Meghan's heart. She fell in love instantly, the same way she fell for Ralph - *instantly.* As he walked over to her, she admired his swagger. She could tell that he used to be a hood boy, but he must have gotten rich and got up out of the hood. *His impeccable swagger is definitely off the hook.*

"That's fine." Meghan returned a flirtatious smile. "I was thinking about renting this one anyways." She shrugged her shoulders as she continuously walked around the car and looked inside the car through the glass windows.

"This one is the most expensive car in the lot to rent," he informed her. Before she could ask, he told her the price. "It's $2,000 a day."

Meghan gulped down hard at the price. "That's a lot," Meghan said as she leaned against the car. He thought that she was going to say she didn't want it, that it was too expensive for her budget. "But I'll take it."

"I didn't think you would have that kind of money."

"What are you trying to say?" Meghan cocked her head back. "Are you trying to say I look like I'm broke?"

"No, I'm not saying that," he nervously chuckled. "I apologize…I just never get any females your age coming in here trying to rent a luxurious car." He assured her, "But if this car is the one you want to rent, you're welcome to it."

Meghan couldn't believe he would say that, but she quickly forgave him when he apologized.

"What's your name?"

"Meghan."

"Nice to meet you, Meghan. My name is Jamal." He shook her hand and brought her hand up to his mouth and kissed it while gazing into her eyes. Meghan blushed, gently taking her hand back.

"Um, would you like to take the car for a spin?"

"Sure." Meghan shrugged her shoulders. As she went to go reach for the handle, to her surprise, he stopped her and opened it for her. Meghan never had anyone open up the car door for her - or any door, for that matter.

"What a gentleman!" Meghan complimented him as she slid into the driver's side seat. She watched as Jamal walked around and got into the car and put on his seatbelt.

"What, you never had a man open up the door for you?" he said with a puzzled look.

"No," Meghan answered casually. "Is that something men do around here?"

"Around here?" Jamal smiled. "I could tell you're not from around here," he said as he slid the keys in the ignition and turned on the car. "I don't know about every other man; I can only speak for myself. My mother raised me to the best of her ability, and she raised a gentleman," he assured Meghan.

"Well, back in Boston, never in my life have I encountered a man who opened the door for me. I've never seen anyone do that for a woman."

"You're from Boston, huh?"

"Yup," Meghan smiled. "Born and raised."

"So what made you come here?" Jamal questioned inquisitively.

"Just to get away," Meghan responded nonchalantly as she carefully pulled out of the lot.

Jamal instructed her on where to go and as they drove through Palm Beach, he was giving her a tour of the city. After they chatted and got to know each other while cruising Palm Beach City, they made their way back to his car lot.

Meghan killed the engine, removed the keys, and handed them to Jamal.

"I really enjoyed your company." Meghan smiled as she shrugged one shoulder.

"I enjoyed yours too." Jamal returned a smile, showing off his perfect white teeth. "So, what are you doing tonight?"

Meghan shrugged her shoulders. "I don't know. What is there to do around here?"

"Well, for starters…there is an all-white party tonight," he informed her. "I know you don't know your way around just yet, but I would like you to come."

"Are you asking me to be your date?" Meghan cooed.

"I don't know," he said slyly. "I was going to ask you to be my date." He smiled as he tugged on his chin hairs, staring at Meghan from the side.

Meghan smiled and sighed loudly. "I don't know." She shrugged her shoulders. "I'm still sitting here and you still didn't ask me," she said sarcastically.

"Will you be my date for tonight?" he said as he turned around to face her.

"Yes, I will be your date for tonight," Meghan agreed. "What's the address?"

"Don't worry about the address," he informed her as he pulled out his phone. "I'll have my limo pick you up around eight."

"What about my friends?"

"No biggie; they can come too," he said as he typed in the passcode to his phone. "What's the address to where y'all are staying?"

"I'm staying at the Chesterfield Hotel," she informed him. He looked up from his phone and pursed his lips together, bobbing his head.

"Oh, so you like luxurious cars and extravagant hotels." Jamal cracked a smile. "High class." He typed something down on his phone.

"I wouldn't say I'm high class, but I like the finer things in life." She bobbed her head slightly, agreeing with him. Who wouldn't love having luxurious things? She came from the hood and that's what she wished she had.

"I hear that. You're just like me." He winked. "Here, take down my number and call me when you and your girls get ready."

Meghan took out her cell phone and programmed in his number as he told it to her. He opened up the door to get out, walking around the hood of the car with one hand resting in his pocket. Meghan turned to her left. Jamal bent down and said,

"Make sure you and your girls wear all white." He winked.

"Got ya," Meghan said as she grabbed the handle, about to open the door.

"Don't worry about paying for the rental. It's on the house." He winked. "Just be ready at 8:00."

"Okay." Meghan blushed. "Thank you, Jamal. I truly appreciate what you're doing. How can I ever repay you for this?"

"Just be ready at 8:00 and maybe we can go on a second date…that's if I like you," he said jokingly as they both chuckled for a few seconds.

"I guess I'll see you at 8:00, and you better have your check ready for our second date." Meghan winked before placing the car in drive and pulling off. She stared in her rearview mirror, looking back at Jamal, who was standing there with a smile. Meghan made it to the hotel within minutes, tossing the keys to the valet.

Meghan didn't have time to wait for the elevator. She was so excited for tonight. She quickly ascended the stairs. As soon as she reached the penthouse, floor she was out of breath. Walking to her room, she slid the key in the door and opened it up. Breathing heavily, she walked in and plopped on the couch next to Carmen, who was looking in the Yellow Pages.

"Damn, girl, what, is someone chasing you?" Carmen's eyes never left the book.

"No." Meghan laughed. "I got invited to an all-white affair tonight, and y'all are also coming," Meghan said excitedly as she watched Nicolette emerge from the room rubbing her eyes. Her hair was unruly.

"Who invited you?" Nicolette asked as she sat down on the chair.

"A handsome man named Jamal." Meghan started to blush. "He's having a limo pick us up at 8:00, so you know what that means…"

"SHOPPING!" they all screamed in unison.

Nicolette

Nicolette scanned the racks in a Boutique called Lily's Boutique, which the girls had stumbled upon while cruising the streets of Palm Beach. Meghan and Carmen were in the glasses section trying on expensive shades. Nicolette slid the clothes to the side as she scanned the racks, looking for something nice to wear to the party. She looked over her shoulders and quickly unzipped the purse she had hanging off her shoulder. She snatched several dresses off the rack and stuffed them into her purse.

Nicolette looked around and noticed no one had noticed what she had just done. She then looked up and saw a camera pointed directly at her. *Shit!* Nicolette turned her back towards the camera and walked around the store, heading over to more exquisite dresses. *Now this dress right here is more Palm Beach style,* Nicolette said to herself as she grabbed an all-white sleeveless cocktail dress. It had a deep slit on the side where the thigh would be.

Nicolette placed the dress up to her, hugging her body as she turned from side to side, imagining how the dress would look on her. *This dress is perfect!* She read the price tag on the dress and it read $1,387.33. Nicolette rolled her eyes and said to herself, *I do not have that kind of money!* Nicolette discreetly looked over at the older Caucasian gray-haired old woman behind the register. She was smiling as she gradually rang up a customer. Nicolette carefully folded the dress up and stuffed it in her purse along with the rest of the items she had taken.

She nervously looked up and noticed the older woman now staring at her while she had a cordless phone up to her ear. Nicolette gulped down hard, hoping she wasn't calling the police. Nicolette looked around and Meghan and Carmen were nowhere in sight. She didn't want to go around the store searching for them because she felt the woman was onto her the way she was eyeballing her. Nicolette had a tight grip on her purse as she walked past the racks and headed for the front door.

She noticed a blue and white police car pulling up. It said **"POLICE"** on the top and **"Palm Beach"** right below it. *SHIT!* Nicolette thought to herself. She had to keep calm and collected as she emerged from the boutique. Nicolette licked her lips nervously as she pushed the door open. She swept her blonde hair behind her ear and started walking at a quick pace.

"Ma'am," a police officer called out, but Nicolette purposely disregarded him. "Ma'am, can I talk to you for one second?" the officer called out again.

Nicolette stopped in her tracks and squeezed her eyes shut for several seconds before opening them back up again. She knew she had to stop because she feared that if she kept walking, he would have shot her right in the back. She didn't know about the police in Palm Beach, but Boston was a different story. Nicolette turned around and gulped down hard. He gradually walked over towards her with his arm resting on his gun.

"Yes, officer?" Nicolette acknowledged him nervously as she had a tight clutch on her purse with the stolen goods inside.

"I got a phone call about someone stealing out of Lily's Boutique," he said, "And you fit the description." He stared into her luminous blue eyes. "Let me see the bag," he asked as he extended his hand.

Nicolette rolled her eyes, causing a tear to escape and trickle down her cheek. Sighing dejectedly, she reluctantly handed over the bag. She folded her arms across her breasts as she ran her tongue across her top teeth, tapping her foot impatiently on the sidewalk. She watched as he pulled one long extravagant gown out of her purse and held it up into the air, revealing the dress she had stolen.

"I've seen enough," he said.

Nicolette didn't put up a battle. She knew was responsible for stealing and she now had to be penalized. Voluntarily, she extended both of her arms, waiting for handcuffs to be placed on her wrist. Nicolette watched as he turned around and walked towards his car. She placed down her arms with a baffled facial expression plastered on her face. He walked to his police car and opened up the back door for her, signaling her with his hand to get in. For a second she thought she was off the hook.

Nicolette dragged her feet as tears escaped her eyes, knowing she was about to go to jail for shoplifting. Before she stepped foot into the car, she looked towards the boutique and noticed Meghan and Carmen at the register paying for their stuff. Carmen tapped Meghan on the shoulder and pointed towards the glass window. Shock was written across both of their faces as they watched Nicolette being escorted into the back seat of a patrol car. She watched as he walked into the boutique and stayed there for several seconds before coming back out. She wondered what the old woman had told him, and she also wondered why he didn't take back the clothes she had stolen. He hopped in the car and Nicolette quickly put her head down in shame as the police officer drove off. After driving for several minutes, Nicolette wiped away her fresh, salty tears and held up her head. She noticed the officer sneaking peeks at her through his rear view mirror.

"So what's a beautiful young lady like yourself stealing for?"

Silence filled the car, but he had just broken it with his odd question. Nicolette's eyebrows arched up as she stared at him through the rearview mirror. *You've got to be kidding me,* she thought to herself. Nicolette wasn't going to answer the question, but she did anyways. "I needed something to wear tonight," Nicolette admitted.

"Where are you going?"

"To some all-white party my friend got invited to," Nicolette informed him as she looked out the window. She couldn't believe she was in this predicament.

"Where do you live?"

"What's up with all of the questions?" Nicolette barked.

"It's your choice whether or not to answer my question," he replied smartly, "You decide your own fate by answering one simple question."

Nicolette stared at him intensely through the rearview mirror, wondering what kind of game this cop was playing. He stared back at her, gazing into her blue eyes from the mirror. Nicolette turned away quickly, trying to hide the smile she was wearing on her face.

"The Chesterfield Hotel." Nicolette looked out the window. He laughed. She then turned and looked at him. "What's so funny, officer?"

"Oh, nothing, besides the fact that you're staying at a hotel - and an expensive one a that." She knew exactly what he was getting at too by saying "an expensive one at that".

"I know what you're thinking. I'm not the one paying for the hotel. Of course if I had money, I wouldn't be shoplifting, now would I?" Nicolette asked with a stern face and her arms folded across her breasts.

"I guess." He shrugged his shoulders as he put on his signal and turned right. "Where are you from anyways?" Before she could answer, he continued talking. "I have never seen you around here and I'm a cop, so I know a lot of people in Palm Beach."

"I'm from Boston," Nicolette said casually.

"That's why you're staying in a hotel?"

Nicolette rolled her eyes, getting agitated with his consecutive questions. "Listen, I'm not trying to be rude," Nicolette stated, "But why the hell do you keep asking me these questions? You don't give a damn about me. You're just going to lock me up for some petty shoplifting charge and make me sit in a jail cell. Hey, I might even get jumped in jail just because a cop decided to take me to jail for something so petty. I don't even know why the hell you're asking." Nicolette stopped in her tracks as she noticed the officer pulling up in front of Chesterfield Hotel.

"You're free to go." He pushed the gear stick into park as the police car jerked forward.

Nicolette looked at the officer and said, "You're letting me go?"

"For now," he replied smartly as he got out of the car, holding her bag in his hand. He opened up the back door for her and she got out. He held his hand out, gesturing for her to take her bag.

"I don't want that stuff," Nicolette said referring to the stolen items. "I'd just like my bag back," she admitted truthfully.

"It's okay. Take it," he said, pushing the bag towards her.

Nicolette grabbed the bag slowly, staring him in the eyes. She was wondering why he was being so generous to her, especially since she had just stolen several thousand dollars worth of clothes. "I shouldn't. What I did was wrong." Nicolette shook her head and tried to hand the back to him, but he wouldn't accept it.

"Don't worry about it," he said as he gently shoved the bag into her arms. "My name is Officer Porter, but you can call me John," he said as he pulled out a card and handed it to Nicolette. "I'll be seeing you around." He tilted his police hat, walked around the hood of the police cruiser, and got into his car.

Nicolette bit down on the bottom of her lip as she looked down at the card. It was his own custom business card. *Where they do that at?* Nicolette thought to herself as she looked up and watched as he slowly drove away. Nicolette wasn't too fond of cops, but she actually liked this one. She didn't know what kind of cop would let her go, especially after she had stolen several thousand dollars worth of extravagant clothing, and then drop her back off at her destination. He was decent-looking for a cop. Nicolette actually thought he was very good-looking for a cop.

Although he had his head shaved entirely bald like an older man, he still looked young in the face. She guessed he was in his mid-twenties. He was a Caucasian male, with light blue eyes. His face was freshly-shaved and he resembled Vin Diesel a little bit.

The police uniform he wore was tight, but his muscular arms poked out the sides. He looked like a superhero cop.

She slid his card inside her back pocket and turned around, heading inside the hotel. Once she had gotten inside the penthouse, she headed straight to her side. Nicolette plopped the bag with the stolen goods on the bed and unzipped it. She pulled out each dress, admiring how beautifully made they were. Nicolette was so busy admiring the eloquent gowns that she didn't even hear the front door open. Several seconds later, Meghan and Carmen were behind her. The sound of dropped keys startled her, causing her to turn around swiftly.

"What the hell? You scared me!" Nicolette shrieked as she held her fast-beating heart.

"Why the fuck did you steal clothes from that store, Nicolette?" Meghan asked with a stern voice, her hands on her hips, indicating that she was beyond infuriated.

"Because I have no money, Meghan." Nicolette sat down on the edge of the bed.

"I could have given you some money, Nicolette. That's why we went shopping - so we can find an outfit for tonight - and I was going to pay for it with the money I stole from Ralph...duh!" Meghan smacked her forehead lightly, shaking her head at Nicolette.

"I'm sorry." Nicolette's voice cracked as she broke down crying.

Meghan and Carmen looked at each other for a quick second before tending to Nicolette.

"What's wrong?" Meghan rushed over and sat down by her side and Carmen followed suit. She wrapped her arms around Nicolette's shoulder.

"My mother is dead." She sobbed uncontrollably. The girls had no idea her mother has passed away and they wondered why she hadn't told them.

"What? When?" Meghan asked in disbelief.

"Yesterday, after I left the diner with you guys." Nicolette wiped her face with a piece of Kleenex Carmen had just handed her.

"I'm so sorry for your loss." Meghan squeezed her tighter.

"Me too, sorry for your loss," Carmen added in.

"I just went home, and my aunt and her husband were there. She was crying and all he would tell me is…my mother…" Nicolette sniffled. "I went to the back room and my sister Camilla was there by her side, and she told me she was dead." Nicolette tried to hold back the tears, but she couldn't. The girls didn't know what to say. They felt extremely bad that she had just lost her mother. They couldn't fathom the pain she had endured. They could only imagine.

"I'm okay though," Nicolette lied as she wiped away her tears. "I just have to be strong, knowing she would want me to be."

"So your mother didn't leave you anything?" Meghan asked inquisitively.

"The only thing she left me was $1,000." Nicolette chuckled in disbelief. "Could you believe that? Before my mother passed away, she reassured me that I would be good if she died. And I know for a fact that my mother wouldn't just leave me $1,000. I know my sister is lying."

"Why would she lie about that?"

Nicolette shrugged her shoulders. "I don't know. She probably killed her."

"Don't say that! She wouldn't kill your mother."

"You don't know my sister!" Nicolette retorted. "What my mother did to her…she would never forgive her. She had motive."

"How did she die?" Carmen asked inquisitively.

"I don't know," Nicolette said with arched brows. She didn't know the exact cause of her death. "My sister said that her cancer had come back, when clearly the doctors announced that it went away. I just assumed she died from the cancer." She shrugged her shoulders. "I don't know, but she's dead, and this conversation isn't going to bring her back. I'm done." Nicolette rose to her feet as she removed her cell phone from her back pocket. "Excuse me;

I have a phone call to make." She stormed out of the room, her long blonde hair swinging back and forth as she stormed out of the penthouse.

Carmen

Riding around in the front seat of Meghan's Maybach rental, windows down, her crimson-colored hair blew wildly with the wind. Carmen stared out the window, smiling from ear to ear as they pulled up into a luxurious neighborhood. They all gawked at the beautiful houses that were all closed off with beautiful gates. Carmen couldn't believe how beautiful these houses were. She knew for sure that these houses cost a lot of money - money that neither she nor her girls could afford. Carmen pointed out the car that the real estate agent said he would be driving. Meghan took a right onto a granite path, slowing down and pulling up behind the real estate agent's all-black Rolls Royce.

After killing the engine, Carmen hopped out of the car with her girls. Carmen looked around, examining the exterior of the house before proceeding up the stairs. Before Carmen could ring the doorbell, the front door slowly opened up. There was a handsome man standing there before her eyes. His face was so smooth besides the stubbly area on the lower part of his face. His eyes were a greyish-hazel color and they were sparkly. When he smiled, he revealed his perfect pearly-white teeth. He was wearing all-black jeans and a white button-up that was unbuttoned several buttons, showing off several hairs on his chest. His jet-black hair was slicked back with no hair out of place. Carmen loved her some Puerto Rican men, and he was just her type.

"Hi, are you Carmen?"

"Yes. We're here to see the house." She smiled as she extended her hand to shake his. He grabbed her hand and lowered his head, kissing her hand with his succulent lips, sending chills down her body. Carmen blushed as she took back her hand and stepped inside of the house. He greeted the other girls and closed the door behind them. Although Carmen didn't have the money to even put down towards a house, she wanted to make it appear like she was the one in charge. Especially since he was a good looking man, she wanted to put on a good impression. He walked around the entire house, showing them every aspect of it. It had four bedrooms, four baths, a Jacuzzi room, and a huge living and dining room. Throughout the entire time he showed them around the house, Carmen had her eyes fixed on him.

"How much does this house go for?" Meghan asked curiously as she ran her French tips across the marble kitchen countertops.

"$600,000," he spoke casually with his hands in his back pocket.

Meghan shook her head, "Excuse me; let me talk to my girls." Meghan excused her self. Carmen smiled as she excused herself as well. She walked into the living room behind Meghan and Nicolette.

"I don't have that type of money," Meghan muttered, "We don't have that type of money." Meghan stated referring to all of them. Carmen looked over at the realtor and gave him a friendly gesture, pretending like everything was okay.

"When I thought you said you was going to look for an affordable apartment, I didn't think you would look for a fucking expensive house like this," Meghan said with her hands wandering in the air.

"I'm sorry," Carmen apologized. "I didn't know this house was that much either. I called a few other real estate agents but he was the only available that could show us something today Sorry," Carmen apologized again.

"It's okay," Meghan assured her as she touched her shoulder, pushing her towards the kitchen, where the real estate agent was walking back and forth in the kitchen.

"Listen, what's your name?" Meghan asked.

"Romeo."

"Listen, Romeo…" Meghan scratched her head. "Do you have any apartments that are around one thousand dollars a month or maybe fifteen hundred? We can't afford this," Meghan stated bluntly.

Carmen was slightly embarrassed. Although the price he had told them was a lot of money, she wanted Romeo to believe she could afford it.

"No, I'm sorry. I don't sell those type of properties. I only sell the best houses there are in Palm Beach - extravagant ones, that is," he informed them with a smile.

"Thanks for your help anyway." Carmen smiled and had turned to walk away when he stopped her.

"Look, I know a few people who probably have some units coming up, but it probably won't be for the next couple of months."

"Well, that's just great." Meghan said sarcastically as she held her hand up and smacked her thigh. Meghan walked out of the house with Nicolette following closely behind her.

"Okay, thanks, Romeo, I appreciate it. I'll be in touch." Carmen turned to walk away again, but this time Romeo grabbed her hand.

"I would like to call you some time."

"You're married," Carmen said, eyeing the ring he rocked on his wedding finger.

He chuckled nervously as he slid the ring off his finger. "No, not anymore." He shook his head as he stared at the ring and slid it into his pocket. "We got a divorce. I was just so used to wearing the ring that I never took it off." Romeo stared at Carmen and licked his bottom lip. "This is the first time," he said, referring to taking off the ring.

"I see." Carmen pursed her lips together. "It shows that you're not over her." Carmen walked towards the front door and opened it. Meghan was standing there leaning on the rail while Nicolette smoked on a long Virginia Slim cigarette.

"That's not true," he stated, trying to defend himself. "I'm honestly too busy showing houses all the time. I honestly forgot that I had it on."

"I guess I believe you." Carmen worked up a smile, blushing a little bit. She emerged from the front door and stood next to her friends, turning around to face Romeo.

"There's a party tonight if y'all ladies would like to come. It's an all-white party."

"Well, I already got invited." Meghan smiled from ear to ear, trying to hide the fact that she was blushing.

"May I ask by who?"

"Jamal. He's the owner of Rent A Luxury Car."

"Oh, Jamal." He laughed with his fist covering his mouth. "He moved on already."

"You know him?" Meghan asked as if it wasn't possible that he could know him.

"Of course I know him. He's my best friend," Romeo informed her.

"Do you know the Officer John Porter?" Nicolette asked out of curiosity.

"Of course! Who doesn't know Officer Porter?" Romeo chuckled. "He's a good friend of mine as well. We all moved from Fort Lauderdale while Jamal and I were still stuck living the lifestyle we lived. John joined the force and has been a cop ever since."

"How did you meet John? Not under good circumstances, I bet?" Romeo joked.

Nicolette rolled her eyes and smiled. "Although he's a cop, he seems like he's very caring. He's probably a crooked cop," she joked, and the girls laughed as well.

Romeo chuckled nervously and said, "Well, ladies, I have to show a property to another client." He removed his phone from his pocket and checked a text. "So I should be seeing you later on tonight?" he asked, focusing his eyes specifically on Carmen as he talked.

"Yes, I'll be there."

"See you tonight." He winked at her. He turned around and locked up the house and headed to his car.

Carmen and the girls walked to the car and hopped in.

"He got your panties wet already, huh?" Nicolette cooed as she nudged Carmen's arm from the back seat.

"Oh, please!" Carmen giggled, moving around in her seat. Her friend was absolutely correct because her panties were damp just from looking at him. "He sure is sexy though," Carmen added.

"Is he married?" Meghan questioned as she pulled off.

"No. He was, but he got a divorce."

"You better be careful, because ex-wives are fucking crazy!" Nicolette stated as if she had personally dated a married man.

"How do you know that?"

"Because I just know from Lifetime movies and stuff."

They all busted out into laughter at Nicolette's silly joke. Carmen could only imagine. She just hoped that if she and Romeo became close, his ex-wife wasn't crazy. Carmen couldn't wait for the all-white party. She would make sure to dress to impress, just for him.

Meghan

Riding in an all-white stretch limousine was the way Meghan pictured it. Sipping on V-shaped glasses of champagne was the epitome of the lifestyle people lived in Palm Beach. Meghan sat in the back seat with Jamal sitting so close to her that she could smell the aroma of Armani cologne emerging from his neck. Jamal had his arms wrapped around Meghan's neck as if he had known her for years. Meghan grew comfortable with him within minutes of meeting him. She didn't know what it was about him. Meghan watched as Jamal stared out the tinted limousine window, tugging at his chin hairs with his free hand. Jamal turned away from the window when he felt Meghan's eyes fixed on him. She smiled and quickly looked away and then noticed the limousine coming to a stop.

Meghan watched as Jamal opened up the door for her, extended his hand, and helped her get out of the car. When she got out, he raised her soft hand up to his thick lips and kissed them. Meghan almost melted inside as she felt his warm, juicy lips touch her soft skin, sending tingles down her spine. She felt like that was a common gesture that he did, and she liked it. He hesitantly let go of her hand, as if he didn't want to. Meghan smiled as she watched her date open up the door for her best friends, as a gentleman should. *He's definitely a keeper.*

Jamal winked at her before interlocking arms with her and they walked down the red carpet. Meghan looked around and noticed there was a long line. Frustrated, she thought they all had to wait in it. Jamal walked past the crowd and straight up to the security guards. They didn't even have to check a guest list. They undid the long hook and a man waved his hand, giving them an okay to enter. Meghan looked back, smiling as she shrugged one of her shoulders at her girls, excited. They were excited as well, and happy they didn't have to stand in that stretch of a line.

Once inside, Carmen and Nicolette went their separate ways from Meghan. She shrugged her shoulders and looked at Jamal, who smiled at her.

"They are fine," Jamal assured her, seeing a sign of nervousness written on her face. She wasn't nervous at all. She just didn't expect them to leave her so quickly. "We need time to bond anyways." He winked at her and grabbed her hand. "Come on."

Meghan's eyes scanned the spacious hall, which was filled to its capacity. Everyone inside looked like they were either rich or knew someone who was. Everyone had on extravagant attire, including the servers and the DJ. For a second, Meghan felt like all eyes were on her and Jamal. An older black man walked up to Jamal and gave him dap, pulling him closely for a quick hug. When the man pulled back from an embrace, the guy smiled at Meghan and shook her hand gently.

"Man, Jamal." The man shook his head. "She is beautiful. I didn't know you got married to this beautiful young lady. Why didn't you tell me?"

Meghan arched her brows, staring at the man, wondering what the hell he was talking about.

Jamal chuckled as he took his hand out of his pocket. "She's not my wife, and I never got married," he assured the man with a friendly gesture. "But you got that right: she sure is beautiful." Jamal looked over at Meghan, who was blushing. She removed a piece of loose hair that was in her face, placing it behind her ear.

"My fault, Jamal," he apologized. "She's a keeper though." He playfully nudged Jamal on the shoulder and kept it moving through the crowd.

"Who was he?" Meghan asked curiously. "And what the hell was he talking about?"

"He's a friend of my father's, and I have no idea. I never came close to marrying a woman. He just thought we looked like a good couple…that's all."

Meghan smiled as they continued to walk through the hall. Meghan silently thanked God. They took a seat, much to her relief. The four-inch red bottoms she had on were killing her feet. Meghan had always been a sophisticated, classy young woman but she had never worn heels before in her life. She was always accustomed to shoes that only had an inch to them, not four.

"Would you like anything to drink?"

"Whatever you're having, I'll have," Meghan insisted with a gracious smile.

Jamal ordered two drinks for them and turned his whole body around in the seat just to look at Meghan. Meghan rubbed her ankles as she turned around and stared into the party.

"Feet hurt already?" Jamal asked.

Meghan smiled and quickly put her foot down and said, "Yeah, you could say that." She nodded her head with a smirk. "I hardly wear heels, and when I do, they are never this high."

"Well, maybe you should have been more comfortable instead of trying to outdo yourself." He picked up his drink that the bartender had just placed down seconds ago.

Meghan stared at him with a "no you didn't" look. Normally Meghan didn't like a man who always joked, but she knew Jamal was a sweet, genuine man with a small sense of humor. She didn't mind; she thought it was actually cute. "Never trying to outdo it; just keeping up with the ladies of Palm Beach," Meghan replied as she picked up her drink and took a sip from it before placing it down. "I knew that everyone here would be dressed to impress, and I know I didn't want to look like an oddball with my street clothes on."

Jamal smiled and tilted his head to the side. "So if that's the case, who are you trying to impress?" Jamal's left eyebrow shot up as he sipped on his alcoholic beverage, waiting for an answer.

Meghan wanted to kick her self inside. She didn't know what the hell she was saying. She just didn't want to come to an extravagant party looking like a hood chick. "You, of course," Meghan said smoothly, eyeing Jamal through the glass as she gulped down the rest of her drink with as much elegance as she could muster.

"Well…" Jamal fiddled his hands around the glass. "It doesn't matter how you're dressed or how you look. You're beyond beautiful, and if it makes you feel better, you don't have to impress a guy like me." He enlightened her with a loving smile. "I'm not like these other guys in here who would judge a woman by what she's wearing. I judge you by what's in here," Jamal said as he gently tapped Meghan's chest, pointing towards her heart.

Meghan smiled and turned her head, hiding the fact that she was blushing very hard. She felt like Jamal always knew what to say and how to make a woman feel good.

"I guess someone is feeling your boy," Jamal said, sounding hood.

Meghan turned around and noticed Jamal looking straight ahead with both his eyebrows arched and a wide smirk on his face. She playfully nudged his shoulder and laughed.

"Well, it seems like I'm not the only one who's blushing." Meghan noticed Jamal was blushing and then he smiled, accentuating the deep dimples that were concealed when he didn't smile. The only time she noticed his sexy dimples was when he talked a certain way or smiled widely.

"Well, I must admit, I haven't blushed in a while. I haven't seen a beautiful woman like you around here – well, at least not my type."

"What's your type?"

"Black, beautiful woman like yourself, very sophisticated, classy with a little bit of hood in her." He indicated *a little* with his index finger and thumb touching. "Too many prissy woman around here, walking around like their shit don't stank…excuse my language." They both chuckled.

"No, you don't have to excuse your language," Meghan assured him as she touched his leg. "I love a little hood in my men as well." She winked at him. "I know a hood man when I see one."

"Well, you can take the man out the hood, but you - "

"Can't take the hood out of the man!" Meghan helped him finish his sentenced as she bobbed her head, smiling. They both broke into a laughter.

"I've been in the streets since I was about fourteen. My parents were always too busy at work. I couldn't blame them." Jamal shrugged his shoulders. "They always kept food in the fridge, clothes on me and my brother's back, gave us everything we ever needed. I just never really appreciated what they did for me. I was introduced to the streets, and all I cared about was that drug money. My father begged me to stay out the streets. He even went so hard to tell me anything I needed was paid for, car paid for. He bought me my first Porsche at age sixteen. My older brother, who was doing well in school, he got nothing. So when my father died, he left me his insurance company to run. I left the streets and never returned to hustling. My brother was so mad that he left me the insurance company. He begged me to sell it to him, but it was bringing in so much money that I couldn't. We eventually ended up going our separate ways."

"What happened?"

"It's a long story." He sighed. "But I caught him trying to steal my money once."

"Wow, that's harsh." Meghan pursed her lips together. "At least you're not in the streets anymore. That's a good thing." She took a sip of her drink.

"Yeah," he said casually. "So enough of me. Let's talk about you," Jamal insisted, "Why did you come to Palm Beach?"

"Like I told you before, I needed to get away. You know," Meghan said, trying to beat around the bush. "My mother didn't want me to move to Palm Beach, but I'm grown and do as I please."

"How old are you, about eighteen?"

"Yeah, why?"

"I left the house at eighteen too. I was running the streets like I knew everything." Jamal chuckled as he reminisced about when he was as hard headed as can be. "I used to live in Fort Lauderdale, but when my business skyrocketed, I decide to pack my things and move myself and the company to Palm Beach, leaving my mother, brother, and other family behind."

After getting to know each other for about an hour and a half, Jamal led Meghan up a spiral staircase which led to hotel rooms. Meghan was twisted from the several glasses of alcohol she consumed. Meghan followed Jamal into a hotel room. She walked over to the bed, sat down on the edge, and took off her heels.

"I need to get used to walking in heels, because seriously…this is ridiculous!" Meghan barked as she rubbed her feet.

Jamal walked over, pulling a chair up to the bottom of the bed, and took one of Meghan's feet in his hands. He started to massage Meghan's feet, sending chills down her spine and through her body with his simple touch.

"May I?" he asked as he stopped massaging her feet.

She bit down on her bottom lip and nodded her head yes. The way he was massaging her feet was amazing. He had hands like no other. Meghan sat up on her elbows and tilted her head back while arching her back. She closed her eyes and enjoyed the way he massaged the hell out of her foot.

Meghan's eyes shot open when she felt a warm sensation wrap around her toes. She looked down and Jamal had her big toe in his mouth, licking it. She was a little taken aback by that. As pretty as her feet were, her ex-boyfriend Ralph would never suck her toes. He acted like it was nasty or something, Meghan didn't even care. She enjoyed it.

Jamal stopped licking her toes and stood up. He climbed on top of the bed, slowly lying on top of Meghan and kissing her neck. Meghan moaned softly in his ear with each lick he inflicted on her neck. She couldn't contain the way she was feeling. She wrapped her arms around his neck. As he sucked on her neck, she sucked on his earlobe. Her panties started to get wet the more he licked and sucked on her neck. Meghan was sure she had an enormous hickey on her neck by now with the way he was sucking.

Jamal ran his hands along her body and unzipped her cocktail dress. Meghan wiggled her body as Jamal helped her take off her dress. After tossing it to the floor, Jamal stood on the bed on his knees, unbuckling his white-collared shirt, and then he took off his slacks and boxers. Tossing them to the floor, he wasted no time getting back to kissing her neck. Meghan loved the way his naked body felt pressed against her silky skin. She tightened her pussy muscles as Jamal's dick pressed against her and she felt it growing hard instantly.

Meghan watched as he revealed a condom in his hand. He opened the package, and slid it on his dick. He gripped his dick and rubbed it on her clit up and down, making her super wet. Meghan loved the way that felt when he did that. He wasn't rough either. He was doing it nice and soft, so gentle she nearly came. She bit down on her lip to avoid screaming as he slid his enormous dick inside of her and went to work. Meghan just laid there in the zone as he did all of the work. She enjoyed how he felt inside of her. *Even Ralph couldn't lay it down like this,* Meghan thought to herself as Jamal pumped in and out of her.

"Ohhh, Jamal!" Meghan moaned his name as he slowed up the pace.

Meghan felt like he was making love to her with the way he was whispering in her ear. Meghan came shortly after she felt a change in the way his dick felt, like it was warmer. She didn't even notice that he had taken off the condom in the midst of them making love.

They changed positions and Meghan was now on top of Jamal. Clutching onto a good portion of her straight hair, she rode him slowly. Jamal had a firm grip on her waist and started to bounce her up and down. The way she was riding him felt so good, but he encouraged her to go faster as her ass continuously bounced on his legs. Jamal closed his eyes, curled his toes, and moaned loudly as he felt himself about to come. Meghan released her hands from her hair and wound her hips, moving her lower body around in circles, causing Jamal to nut within seconds. All sweaty and exhausted, Meghan collapsed on his chest and stared up at him.

“I never experienced this before,” Meghan admitted. “I never felt so good.”

“Me neither,” Jamal said as he gently rubbed her hair in a backwards motion.

Meghan lifted her leg and removed herself off of him. She looked down and noticed he didn’t have a condom on. A baffled facial expression appeared on her face. Her eyebrows arched up, causing several wrinkles to appear on her forehead. “What happened to the condom you had on?”

“It broke,” Jamal said casually as he apologized. “I didn’t want to stop because it felt so good,” he admitted as he nervously bit down on his bottom lip. “I’m sorry…”

“It did feel good though.” Meghan chuckled nervously as she got up, pulling the sheets off the bed. She headed into the bathroom. Meghan turned on the shower water and dropped the sheets, revealing her naked, voluptuous body. She stepped in the shower, letting the warm water hit every inch of her body. Within seconds, Jamal slid back the shower curtain and stepped inside with her.

“Are you mad at me?”

“Mad at you for what?” Meghan looked back as she washed her body with a clean bar of soap the hotel had supplied.

“For not stopping, since the condom broke.”

“No, I’m not mad,” Meghan said as she turned around and wrapped her arms around Jamal. “It felt too good to stop.”

Meghan placed her lips on his and kissed him passionately as their wet bodies rubbed against each other. They went for a second round in the shower, exploring each other’s bodies. Jamal was the second man whom Meghan had ever had sex with. She had lost her virginity to Ralph, but she felt like Jamal just took her virginity all over again. Meghan was already falling quickly for Jamal. In her eyes, he was Mr. Right.

Nicolette

As Nicolette sat at the bar sipping on a tall Cotton Candy cocktail, she felt a pair of eyes staring her down. Slightly looking over her shoulders, she noticed Officer Porter walking towards her, instantly reminding her of their first encounter.

"Oh no, not him again," Nicolette said out loud as she rolled her eyes. She took a sip of her cocktail and slammed the empty glass down on the counter.

John walked over to her dressed in an all-white tuxedo with a black bow tie. His bald head shone underneath the fluorescent lights that were fixed over the bar section. He slid onto the stool next to her.

"What, are you here to arrest me?" Nicolette asked with such sarcasm that it made him laugh a little bit. She fiddled with her fingers.

"If I wanted to arrest you, I would have arrested you earlier this morning," he informed her with a little sarcasm of his own.

Nicolette laughed for a second. "So what are you here for?" Nicolette didn't even let him answer. "Here to issue me court papers?" Nicolette raised her index finger in the air. "I know…did that old lady decide to press charges against me?" Nicolette asked bluntly.

"No," John spoke casually. "That old lady did not press charges against you. I convinced her not to."

"And why in the world would you do that?" Nicolette finally looked at him, waiting for an answer.

"Because that old lady is my mother and she owns that store."

Nicolette's heart dropped. She couldn't believe the boutique she stole from belonged to his mother. She covered her mouth. "Oh my God, I'm so sorry!" Nicolette apologized, "First thing in the morning I will return everything that I stole, including the dress I have on." Nicolette shook her head and placed her head down, ashamed.

"It's okay," John rubbed her hand, which was lying on the counter. "Keep them. They are already paid for." John smiled.

"How can I ever repay you?"

"First you can let me take you out to dinner tomorrow night and we can talk about how you can really pay me back for stealing from my mother's store."

"Sounds like a plan to me." Nicolette shrugged her shoulders. She assumed she didn't have a choice. "I'm really sorry about stealing from your mother's store. It's just that I just moved here from Boston. My mother passed away and she didn't leave me with anything." Her eyes began to fill up with tears. "I'm so sorry." Nicolette started crying, ruining the makeup Carmen had done for her.

John wrapped his arms around her and rubbed her back as he consoled her. He felt bad for her, and deep down inside, he wanted to help her.

John removed his arms from around her and grabbed his cell phone as it vibrated in his pocket. Nicolette sniffled, wiping away her tears as she watched him answer his phone call. He stood up with one hand in his slacks and the other holding his cell phone.

"Excuse me for one second." John held up one finger in the air, excusing himself.

Nicolette propped up her chin with her hand, watching as John exited the party. Several minutes went by and she became bored. Meghan and Carmen were nowhere in sight, so she decided to go outside to smoke a cigarette. Once outside, she removed her pack of Virginia Slim cigarettes and a lighter from her purse. She removed one from the box, placing it between her lips and lighting it before placing the contents back inside. Her four inch stilettos clicked across the concrete as she made her way over to the banister overlooking the beach. Nicolette took a long drag on the cigarette, tilted her head back, and blew the smoke out of her parted lips.

"The water is beautiful, isn't it?" a voice from behind her said.

For a second, Nicolette thought it was John, but she turned around and it was some Caucasian male dressed in white who appeared to be drunk.

"It is beautiful," Nicolette agreed as she turned around, staring out into the waters, continuously smoking her cigarette.

"You know, you're way too beautiful to be smoking," he chuckled, slurring his words.

Nicolette shrugged and smiled, not knowing what to say. He then moved in closer to her and caressed the side of her face with his middle and index finger. She jumped as he touched the side of her face and it sent unpleasant chills down her spine. Nicolette didn't say anything. She just moved to the side and continued to take long drags on her cigarette, ignoring him.

"I never seen you around here. You new in town?" he asked as he stepped closer to Nicolette, making her anxious.

She didn't know why he kept getting close to her, but she didn't like it one bit. She just wished he would leave her alone already. "Yup," she spoke casually, trying to avoid eye contact with him. But it was hard when he was now standing so close to her. She turned and looked at him. "What do you want?" She stared into his deep blue eyes. He was so close to her face that she could smell the strong stench of liquor on his breath.

"I want you," he whispered seductively. Without notice, he grabbed the back of her head and started to kiss her on her lips as he groped her.

Nicolette dropped the cigarette to the ground and tried to push her head back to avoid prolonging the unexpected kiss. She tried to push him off of her, but her petite frame was no match for the muscular arms that were pinning her down.

"Get off of me!" Nicolette managed to free her hands from him and she started hitting him with her purse, but he didn't flinch. He was trying his hardest to pin down her hands, which were swinging wildly in the air. She was managing to get some hits in. He had managed to pull on her dress, causing a deep rip in it. He forced her against the side of the building where no one could see them.

"Come on, you know you want this," he whispered into her ear and then he licked her earlobe.

Nicolette kept swinging with all her might, but she just couldn't fight him off her. She finally gave in as tears escaped her blue eyes and ruined her mascara. He managed to rip her panties off with one forceful tug, tossing them behind him. The man pulled out his hardened shaft and right before he was about to put it inside of her, a loud gunshot erupted, echoing in the air.

BOOM!

The guy quickly stuffed his junk back into his pants and tried to make a run for it. Nicolette watched as John appeared out of nowhere with his weapon drawn. He chased after the guy and tackled him down to the ground. Nicolette wiped away her tears and slowly slid down to the floor as she watched John forcefully grab the man's arms, bringing them behind his back. He removed a set of handcuffs quickly from his back pocket and tossed them around the man's wrists tightly, causing the man to shriek. John read him his rights.

"Are you alright?" John asked Nicolette as he yanked the guy up to his feet.

"I'm okay." She sniffled as she stood up.

Out of nowhere, a Palm Beach police cruiser showed up and a man got out of the car. John recognized his partner, Officer Hirschberg.

"This is the guy we got a phone call about, huh?" Officer Hirschberg asked as he walked over to John and the guy who tried to rape Nicolette.

"I just came out here and saw what he was doing. I didn't know other reports were made," John said as he pushed the guy towards his partner's cruiser.

"Yeah, some woman in the party called and said this guy had too many drinks and was feeling up on several women." Officer Hirschberg grabbed the man's shoulder, jerking him back and forth lightly. "You like touching women when they don't want you to, huh? Well, there are plenty of people who will sure enough like to touch up on you when you go to jail," he assured him as he opened the door and tossed him in the back of the cruiser. "Are you okay, Miss?" he asked, looking at Nicolette. She was crying and a little shaken up.

"I'm fine," she sniffled, wiping away her tears.

"I'll take it over from here," he informed his partner, giving him a wink. Without another word, his partner hopped in his cruiser, threw on his lights, and drove off.

"Did he - "

Nicolette instantly interrupted John. "No, you came right before he could rape me." Nicolette swept her hair unruly hair back, removing it from her face. "Thank you, Officer Porter. You're a life saver." She worked up a smile.

John took off his blazer and tossed it over her naked shoulders. "Let's go." He placed his arms around her, pulling her closer to him.

"Um, can you take me back to the hotel?" Nicolette stopped in her tracks as she noticed they were heading back to the front entrance of the party. "I look a hot mess, I have no panties on, and plus he ripped the dress I have on." She held onto her long hair as she twisted her body to the side, trying to see the huge rip that was alongside of her leg.

"Sure." John led Nicolette to his car and opened up the door for her, helping her get inside. "Do you want to press charges against him?"

"No…no I don't want to do that," Nicolette spoke quickly. "I'm perfectly fine. He barely touched me," Nicolette lied. She had flashbacks of the way the man groped her and touched her inappropriately, causing tears to reappear in her eyes. She turned her head, quickly blinking them away, so John wouldn't notice her crying. She thanked God that he did show up, because if he had never interrupted the situation, the man would have raped her without any remorse.

Nicolette turned towards him and placed her hand on top of his on the shifter. "I really want to thank you once again. It's just weird how we first met." She chuckled, "You would think you would lock me up, but here you are saving me from being raped by some pervert. What are you, some type of superhero cop or something?" They both busted out into laughter.

"I wouldn't say a superhero cop, more like a friendly cop who doesn't mind doing good deeds for people once in a while," he informed her.

"What about bad deeds?"

John looked at her and didn't bother answering her question. Several minutes later he pulled up in front of the Chesterfield Hotel. "So are you still going to let me take you out for dinner tomorrow?"

"I have no choice. I owe you." Nicolette smirked as she grabbed the handle to the door and stepped out. "I'll call you tomorrow." She waved as she watched his police cruiser slowly pull off. Nicolette sighed as she headed up stairs to the penthouse suite.

Taking off the ruined, expensive dress was the first thing she did when she got upstairs. Then she got in the shower, scrubbing off her body as if it was filthy. She even washed her lips since the guy had kissed them, scrubbing off every trace of his DNA. Tears formed in her eyes. She just wished her mother was still alive. The first day in Palm Beach and she was already off to a bad start. She really hoped that she would soon grow accustomed to living in Palm Beach soon to find her Prince Charming.

Carmen

Carmen looked around the entire hall for Nicolette, but she was nowhere in sight. As soon as she decided to text her, her cell phone chimed, indicating she had received a new notification. Carmen removed the phone from her small white knuckle clutch, sliding her screen to the side. She had received a text from Nicolette saying, "*Sorry I had to leave the party early, I wasn't feeling too good. I'm back at the hotel.*" She smiled as she said a quick prayer, thanking God that she was okay. She had started to panic when she saw her at the bar one minute and then the next minute she was gone and nowhere in sight. She texted back, "*Thank God you're alright! Feel better.*" Carmen pressed the send button before slipping her cell phone back into her clutch.

Carmen decided to go to the bar to get something to drink. After she ordered a margarita, she turned around, leaning against the bar with both of her elbows resting on it. A lot of eyes were on Carmen as she sipped on her margarita. Even men who were with their wives would discreetly sneak a glance at Carmen. All Carmen could do was smile and shake her head at the men who tried to talk to her, who were clearly with other women. She couldn't blame them. She knew she was a sexy, hot Puerto Rican woman that men just couldn't resist.

Carmen was wearing a tight, plain, but cute sleeveless drawstring soft dress with a high neckline. The dress hugged her voluptuous shape, accentuating every curve in her body. She had a beautiful caramel skin complexion and long hair that was naturally curly. Her crimson-colored hair was parted in the middle and bone straight. She wore oversized gold bamboo earrings. A thick herringbone necklace adorned her neck and gold bangles filled her wrist. Ruby red lipstick stained her full, plump lips. Her face was beautifully decorated with MAC brand makeup. That was the good thing about being a makeup artist: you could do your own makeup.

A smile appeared across Carmen's face when she spotted Romeo across the hall. He was looking so handsome in his all-white Armani tuxedo and black tie. Instantly her jaw dropped when she noticed a woman throwing a red-colored drink on him, staining his tux. She watched as the woman stormed away. Romeo looked down at his tuxedo in disbelief, removing a handkerchief from his tux, attempting to remove the stain. That's when Carmen made her move, walking across the hall. Her red pumps clicked ferociously across the shiny floors.

"Are you okay?" Carmen asked.

Romeo stopped wiping his shirt and looked up at Carmen and smiled. "Yeah." He chuckled as he tossed the handkerchief in the trash.

"Is that your ex-wife?" Carmen asked curiously.

"Yeah, that crazy lady is just upset." He sucked his teeth and removed his tuxedo jacket. The shirt underneath had a red stain on it as well.

"Yeah, she must have been really upset," Carmen chuckled, eyeing his shirt.

"I need to go upstairs and change."

"Do you mind if I come?"

"I sure don't." He smiled as he led the way up the spiral staircase to his hotel room. She stood behind Romeo as he removed his hotel card from his pocket, sliding it into the card slot in the door. He opened up the door for her and closed it behind them without locking it. Carmen clutched her purse with a smile, watching him struggle with the buttons on his shirt.

"Let me help you with that." Carmen walked over towards the bed and dropped her clutch onto the bed. She walked over to Romeo and helped him unbutton his shirt.

"I hate button-ups," he admitted as he unloosened the tie from his neck. "I only wear them on special occasions and sometimes for work. They make me look good," he said arrogantly.

"You're not lying about that." Carmen finished unbuttoning his shirt while staring up at him. The way he stared back into her eyes sent chills down her spine. She didn't know what it was and couldn't explain what was happening. She quickly looked away. She unbuttoned the last button and sighed. "All done." Carmen eyeballed his chiseled chest. She gulped down hard as she slowly touched his six pack. She quickly removed her hand from his chest and apologized.

"It's okay; no need to apologize," Romeo informed her. He removed his shirt and then tossed it onto the bed. She didn't notice the stain on his white slacks until she noticed him taking them off. Carmen was stuck in a trance as she eyeballed Romeo getting undressed. She felt like she was watching a movie with the way her eyes were glued to him. She could see a big bulge in the white Polo briefs he was wearing. *Damn, he is packing!* Carmen said to herself. He looked like one of those male models that poses in magazines with his hair slicked back.

"Like what you see?" he spoke in a low and seductive tone.

Carmen quickly snapped out of her trance and shook her head. She was too caught up with staring at him and she didn't notice that he was looking at her. "I'm so sorry!" Carmen chuckled as she covered her mouth. "I just never seen a man with a body like yours before," she admitted.

"You know, I like to work out." He flexed his muscles.

Carmen snickered like a little girl as she playfully slapped his muscular arms. "You're so silly!"

"You're so beautiful," Romeo complimented her while staring deeply into her eyes.

Carmen didn't know what had gotten into her, but her panties were on fire and she wanted a piece of him. She threw herself onto him. Both of her hands gripped the back of his head as they indulged in a passionate kiss. Romeo scooped her up with his arms under her big butt. Carmen moaned as he removed his lips from hers and started sucking passionately on her neck as if he was sucking the juice out of a fresh mango. He laid Carmen gently down on the bed, slid off his briefs, and then removed a condom from the slacks he had discarded on the floor, rolling it onto his shaft. Carmen kicked off her pumps and removed her dress quickly over her head, tossing it to the floor, ruining her straightened hair in the midst of undressing. Romeo wasted no time, getting on the bed and sliding inside of her with one stroke. Carmen clawed at his back, leaving scratch marks from her long, French-manicured tips.

"Damn, you feel so good!" Carmen moaned as he went in and out of her fast and then slowed it down, winding his hips in a circular motion.

Romeo knew by the look on her face that she was loving it. Her eyes rolled into the back of her head as he rocked her world. Changing positions, Carmen sat on top of Romeo and bounced up and down on his nine-inch shaft. She had never seen and felt something so big inside of her. Her mother's boyfriend was nowhere comparable to what Romeo was packing. She gripped her crimson hair tightly as she wound her body on him nice and slow. He grabbed her by the waist and bounced her up and down on his shaft. Carmen hollered out like a maniac as he hit walls she never knew she had. It hurt, but at the same time it felt too good. Carmen was about to nut until Romeo stopped and gently tossed Carmen to the side.

What the hell is going on? She was so busy riding him that she didn't even notice the hotel door had opened. She turned around and swiftly brought the sheets up to cover her nude body.

"While you're in here screwing this bitch," a woman barked as she pointed her hand at Romeo, "you should have been mourning." She sniffled, wiping away her tears before she rushed out of the hotel room.

Baffled, Carmen stood there with her head down, hand rummaging through her hair.

"Marcella!" Romeo yelled out in a heavy Spanish accent. He got up from the bed and quickly slipped back into his briefs.

"Mourning what?"

"Just something we are going through." He shrugged it off.

With arched brows, Carmen folded her arms across her breasts and stared at him with her head tilted. "I thought you guys were divorced."

"We are."

"It don't look like it!" Carmen retorted with an attitude as she removed the sheets from her nude body and slid off the bed.

"She's just going through something and can't get over it that quick," Romeo informed her. He walked over to Carmen and lifted up her chin. "But she's old news," he assured her as he caressed her smooth skin. "I like you, Carmen. You're beautiful, young, and sexy."

Carmen stared into his light hazel eyes, not knowing what else to say. "I like you too, Romeo." Butterflies danced around her stomach as they indulged in a passionate kiss. She couldn't believe she was having sex with a man she barely knew, but she knew deep down inside they had mutual feelings.

Nicolette

The next morning after Nicolette talked to her sister Camilla, she informed her she would be sending her over her money. Although the money from her mother's insurance policy wasn't available yet, she sent her some of her own money instead. Nicolette still didn't believe a thousand dollars was all that was entitled to her, but she shrugged her shoulders and told herself it was better than nothing. After taking a hot shower, she washed her face and brushed her teeth. Nicolette stared in the mirror for several minutes, running her hands through her soft blonde hair, trying to figure out how she would style it. She just decided to tame her hair into a ponytail in the back center of her head. After freshening up in the bathroom, she got dressed, throwing on something casual and then slipping on some sneakers.

Snatching her authentic Louis Vuitton purse off the nightstand, she headed towards the other side of the penthouse. She was going to ask Meghan to borrow the car, but she just decided to walk. She didn't even tell the girls she had almost gotten raped last night. She didn't want them asking her questions and feeling bad for her, so she decided to keep it to herself. Nicolette tiptoed across the penthouse floors, trying not to disturb the girls as they slept. She opened up the door and slowly closed it behind her without making a sound. She took the elevator down to the main lobby and slid on her oversized shades as she emerged from the rotating doors. Nicolette Googled the closet Bank Of America bank in

Palm Beach on her phone. Luckily for her, the bank was exactly two minutes away.

After arriving at the bank, she decided to go to the ATM instead of inside. Removing her ATM card from her purse, she slid it into the machine. Nicolette's eyes lit up when she noticed her sister had transferred over five thousand instead of one thousand. Although she still felt she was entitled to more, she was happy with what she got. She tried to take out a large sum of money, but she forgot she had to take it out in smaller increments. She had to do several transactions before she took out the entire thousand dollars. Nicolette gave up and decided to go inside the bank to get the rest of her money. After receiving her money from the teller, she slipped the envelope in her purse and exited the bank.

She rummaged through her purse, looking for her cell phone. She pulled it out and called her sister. Although she and sister were nowhere near close, she still felt obligated to thank her for sending the money.

"Hey Camilla."

"Hi, Nicolette," she spoke dryly into the phone.

"What's wrong with you?" Nicolette asked as if she cared.

"Oh, nothing, just arranging for Mother's body to be cremated."

"Oh," Nicolette said casually. "I was just calling to say thank you for the money."

"You're welcome. Have a nice life," Camilla said bluntly and then she hung up on her.

Nicolette removed the phone from her ear with her head cocked back in disbelief. She stared at her phone in complete shock. She knew how rude her sister was, but she figured that since their mother died, she could at least cut the bullshit they had going on between them. Nicolette just smiled and shook it off. She didn't care about her sister, and she knew she would never see her again - even better for her. As Nicolette was about to put her cell phone back inside her purse, someone snatched it.

"Hey!" Nicolette screamed as she watched the man take off. "That's my purse!" She stood there for several seconds before she decided to chase after him. She had five thousand dollars in there, and she couldn't let that go without a fight. She chased after the guy, who wore a red hoodie, black jeans, and red sneakers. She didn't know why he was dressed like that because it was hot as hell outside. She picked up her speed and then slowed down when she saw that he had stopped running and taken a right down an alley. Nicolette was furious as she followed him down the alley.

"Hey you!" Nicolette stopped in her tracks when she noticed he had turned around. "Can you please give me my purse back?" she asked politely. "Please?"

The guy walked over to Nicolette, grabbed her by her long ponytail, and swung her to the ground. "You ain't getting shit back!" he barked with a sinister laugh. He removed a pistol from his waistband, revealing it to her.

Nicolette scooted back on the ground and she managed to get up and start running in the opposite direction. She ran for her life as if the mugger was chasing after her. She kept looking over her shoulders to see if he was following her, but he wasn't. Breathing heavily, Nicolette ran into a store, trying to catch her breath.

"Are you okay?" asked an older woman who was shopping with her daughter.

"I'm fine," Nicolette said, trying to catch her breath. "Thank you." Nicolette forced a smile, removing John's business card from her back pocket. She looked down at her phone and as she tapped the numbers, her fingers trembled. Placing the phone up to her ear, she tapped her foot on the floor, patiently waiting for John to pick up. "Pick up…pick up…" Nicolette said through gritted teeth with tears building up in her eyes. Her leg was shaking dramatically as she bit down on her bottom lip, trying to control the tears that were soon to escape her eyes.

"Officer Porter speaking," John answered.

"Hi, Officer Porter." Nicolette tried to sound like nothing had happened, but she broke down into tears. "I need your help. Some guy just robbed me! He stole my purse."

"I'm off duty but, where are you?" he asked, sounding worried.

"I don't know." Nicolette got up and walked outside, telling him what was around her. She assumed he would know since he was a cop and he knew the area.

"I'll be there shortly." He hung up.

Nicolette went back inside to wait for him. Five minutes later, John pulled up in an all black Crown Victoria. It still looked like a cop car to her. Nicolette stood up, exited the store, and walked up to the police cruiser. Although she just had gotten mugged, a smile appeared on her face. She was happy to see him.

"Are you okay?" John asked as he hopped out of the Crown Vic with his hand on his gun, looking around.

"Yeah, I'm fine," Nicolette stated as she swept her hair behind her ear.

"So what happened?"

"I was walking and talking on my phone, and I was about to put my phone in my purse when the next thing you know some idiot snatched my purse and started running." Nicolette shook her head in disbelief and sighed. "I chased after him and he pulled out a gun."

"Alright, let's take a ride." John opened up the passenger side door.

Nicolette smiled, looking at him before getting in the car. "Oh, so you're not going to put me in the backseat?"

"Why would I do that?" John cracked a smile. "This isn't a police cruiser any ways, this is one of my cars for my own personal business." He winked at her and gestured for her to get in with his hand.

Nicolette got in the car and put on her seat belt. She watched as he walked around the hood of the car, looking sexier than he had the other day. She loved the way his muscular arms looked so firm and tight. The police uniform was a little tight, but she had to admit, she loved a man in uniform. She watched him all the way until he got in the car.

"I'm going to drive around and if you see him, point him out to me, alright?"

"Alright." Nicolette stared out the window as he drove off slowly.

Five minutes had passed by and still no sign of the guy who had robbed her. Nicolette perked up and sat up in her seat when she saw a guy wearing a red hoodie from a distance. "That's him…I think that's him right there." Nicolette pointed out the window and slouched down in her seat, not wanting him to see her.

"Stay in the car," John informed her. He had parked several feet away from where the guy was posted up.

Slouched down in the seat, Nicolette watched from the car as John walked over to the guy with his hand resting firmly on his gun. She cracked the window to see what he was saying, but she couldn't hear anything. She watched as John searched him, and several seconds later he returned to the car. With a disappointed look on her face and arms folded across her breasts, she waited for John to come back to the car.

"Why didn't you arrest him?" Nicolette questioned with a baffled facial expression.

"For one, I'm not on duty," he informed her. "I would have call it in…and it wasn't him," he said as he pulled off.

"How do you know that?" Nicolette retorted as she sat up in her seat. "He is the one who robbed me! He snatched my purse and he pulled a gun out on me." Nicolette pierced her eyes at the guy who she knew damn well had robbed her. Tears filled her eyes and she didn't bother wiping them away.

"I searched him and there was no gun on him. He also didn't have anything on him that indicated he had stolen your purse - no money, just an ID and a pack of gum," he informed her.

Everything he was saying went in one ear and out the other.

"That was all I had!" Nicolette turned to look at him. "My sister just sent me money from Boston and that's all I fucking had! What the fuck am I going to do now? Huh, John? I thought you were Super-cop. What happened today?" Nicolette asked bluntly as she kept going on and on. She then realized what he had done for her since she had been in Palm Beach and instantly she felt bad.

"I'm sorry, John." She sighed dejectedly as she ran her fingers through her long ponytail.

"No need to apologize; I understand. But don't worry about it."

Nicolette was about to throw a bitch fit. *Don't worry about it? Don't worry about it? Five fucking grand some guy just stole from me and you're so nonchalant about it.* Was what she wanted to say to John, but she sighed deeply and held it in. Nicolette stared out the window and they pulled up to the Chesterfield Hotel.

"Make sure you're ready tonight by eight."

"For what?" Nicolette had almost forgotten until she remembered they were supposed to go out to dinner that night. She knew she owed him, so she couldn't back down now. She tapped her forehead lightly. "I'm sorry; I almost forgot. I'll be ready at eight."

***

Standing outside the Chesterfield Hotel, Nicolette patiently waited for John to arrive. Several minutes later an all-red Range Rover Sport pulled up with bright blue HIDS lighting up the concrete. Nicolette didn't know if it was John or not so she stood there still looking down the street, expecting him to pull up in a Toyota or something. To her surprise, when the dark-tinted windows rolled down, John was sitting behind the driver's seat with one hand gripping the steering wheel. She didn't know why, but she expected him to pull up in a not-so-expensive car.

"What happened to your other police car lookalike?" Nicolette asked as she slid into the leather seats, closing the door behind her.

"It's at home," he said nonchalantly.

"Not bad for a cop." Nicolette pursed her lips as she eyed the exterior of his car.

"What do you mean not bad for a cop?" he questioned as he turned down the radio. It was playing soft jazz music.

"I mean, I didn't think cops make a lot of money."

"Well, that is true, but I have other sources of income."

"Like what?" Nicolette asked curiously as she peered over at him.

"None of your business." John winked at Nicolette with a devious smirk.

Nicolette's jaw dropped when he said that. She then pursed her lips together, smiling as she bobbed her head.

After a short drive, John announced, "Alright, we are here."

John pulled over perfectly into a parking spot. He got out and opened the car door for Nicolette. They entered the restaurant and didn't have to wait. John already had a private table set up for them. After ordering from the menu, they sat there in silence, waiting for their food.

"So, I barely know anything about you," John broke the silence. "Tell me about yourself."

"What would you like to know?"

"First, why did you come to Palm Beach?"

"Well," she sighed, "my friends and I planned to move here after we finished school, but things happened sooner than we expected. My mother passed away two days ago, so I figured, why not move out here to start off new?"

"I'm sorry to hear that," John said sympathetically. "I can't fathom the amount of pain you're going through. I mean, I lost my dad, but he was hardly in my life. My mother is everything to me. I can only imagine…sorry." He noticed she was getting teary-eyed and caressed her shoulder, trying to comfort her.

"I love my mother. We were very close," Nicolette informed him. "I don't have anything. The only people I have are my friends and the suitcase I rolled in from the airport." She wiped away the tears that escaped her eyes.

"You have me," he assured her as he placed his hand on her hand. He said, "I know we haven't known each other for long, but I know you have a good heart. Whatever you need, just ask."

"Just like that?" Nicolette asked sarcastically, snapping her fingers. "What about a brand new car?" she joked. She smiled when he almost choked on the water he was sipping on.

"Don't push it." They both busted out into laughter.

"I was just kidding." Nicolette took a sip of her iced tea.

"You know you're too beautiful to steal, right?" John said out of the blue, catching her off guard.

At first she didn't know what to say, but she kept it real. "Yeah, I know, but I didn't have any money, and the money that my sister sent me today was all I had. My mother died and my sister told me all my mother left me was $1,000, which is hard to believe, but whatever." Nicolette shrugged her shoulders.

"Well, I know what you're going through and I took it upon myself to get you a few gifts."

"Gifts for me? Already?" She blushed, placing her hand over her chest, flabbergasted.

He nodded his head and excused himself from the table. When he returned, he came back with several bags. He held one big red bag in one hand and two small black bags in the other. Nicolette perked up, sitting up in her seat, wondering what he had brought her. He placed the smaller bags on the table and the larger bag on the floor beside her.

"Go ahead and open them up." John sat back in his chair as he watched Nicolette remove the white tissue paper, removing one of her gifts.

"Since your other one was stolen, I just bought you another one." He took a sip of his water as Nicolette picked up the Louis Vuitton purse, admiring it.

"Thank you! It's even better than my first one." She smiled and placed it back in the bag. She was extremely curious to know what was in the red bag. She pulled several items from it, revealing several extravagant pieces of clothing. "For a cop, you sure know how to pick out some beautiful clothes."

"Well, I have to admit, I am a mother's boy. She always had me picking things out for her boutique and stuff like that. I know what a girl like you likes and wants."

"Oh yeah? So tell me what I want."

"I know you want me," he spoke with certainty, sipping from his drink, still eyeballing her.

"And how in the world would you know that?"

"I was just assuming. I mean, I am a handsome cop, right?" He grabbed his face, massaging it. "I know that I like you – well, from what I see so far."

"So you like a thief? A girl who's broke with nothing?" she asked incredulously.

"Nicolette, that doesn't matter. Everyone makes mistakes. You make mistakes…" He pointed at her. "I make mistakes." He then pointed his index finger towards his chest. "I've been there before. But when you learn from your mistakes, you become a better person. Do I like that you stole from my mother's store? No, but I was willing to give you a chance."

"Well, I appreciate that." Nicolette smiled. She still had one black bag to open. She opened it up and pulled out an envelope that was kind of heavy. "What's this?"

"Open it up and see."

She opened up the envelope and there was a stack of hundred dollar bills sitting in a card. She removed the money from the card and spread the money out. "You didn't?"

"I didn't." He snickered. "I actually arrested the guy who stole your purse. I was cruising the neighborhood later in the day when I started my shift and I got a dispatch that a couple was fighting. I arrested them both and the woman had your bag that her boyfriend had snatched from you."

"Good police work, Officer Porter," she cooed, sounding like a reporter interviewing a cop who had done a good deed. "You really are a superhero cop," Nicolette joked. "No, really, I thank you so much, John. Words can't explain how thankful I am for you."

"You're welcome."

Nicolette continued to dig in the bag and she pulled out a nametag that read ***Lily's Boutique*** at the top in bold and ***Nicolette*** right below it. Before Nicolette could ask him about the nametag, he answered her question.

"I got you a job working at my mother's boutique. She said she wouldn't press charges if you came to work for her. She's even willing to teach you how to sew and make dresses like she does."

Nicolette got up from the table and hugged him, thanking him over and over again. She knew she would feel awkward working there, but she rather work there than go to jail. She couldn't wait to tell the girls she had gotten a job already and she hadn't even been staying in Palm Beach for two days. All she could see were the dollar signs filling her blue eyes. Although she had started off on the wrong foot in Palm Beach, she was making progress now by landing a job. She was thankful and she knew this was truly a blessing in disguise.

Meghan

Meghan hovered over the toilet in their brand new affordable three-bedroom apartment. Meghan held onto the edge of the toilet. Carmen held Meghan's hair back as she vomited into the toilet. It'd been three months since Jamal and Meghan had sex without a condom on. After that day, Jamal used a condom every time. Lately, though, Meghan had started feeling nauseous and she had a lot of morning sickness. For the past few days, Meghan had thrown up every single day in the morning. She couldn't even eat the foods she was used to eating. Meghan didn't know why she was feeling the way she did, but she sure needed to find out. Meghan didn't get to see Jamal too often because he was extremely busy with work. He promised her that he would take her out that weekend, making time just for her.

"Are you pregnant, Meghan?" Carmen asked as she combed Meghan's hair back with her fingers.

Meghan finished throwing up in the toilet and sat up. She moaned as she wiped the side of her mouth with the back of her hand. Ignoring her question, Meghan reminisced on the first night that she and Jamal had sex. She remembered that the condom did break, and he hadn't even informed her that he had taken off the condom after it broke.

"Shit!" Meghan exclaimed.

"Well, are you?" Nicolette prodded as she stood in the doorframe with her arms folded across her breasts, popping her gum loudly.

"I might be," Meghan said casually as she shrugged her shoulders.

"What the hell do you mean, you might be?" Nicolette shot back.

"Well, when Jamal and I were having sex the first time, the condom broke and we just had sex without it."

"And you didn't stop him?"

"I didn't know," Meghan admitted. "I found out after. But it felt so good!" she bragged.

"Better than Ralph?" Nicolette asked curiously.

"Better than Ralph!" Meghan smiled, not even realizing the meaning behind her friend's question. But she shrugged it off and continued talking. "He definitely knows how to put it on a woman," Meghan said, referring to Jamal. Before they could talk any more, Meghan hovered back over the toilet and threw up again. Meghan moaned in pain as the food she ate earlier, came back up. Carmen rubbed her back up and down, trying to comfort her.

"You definitely need to go to the doctor." Carmen helped Meghan to her feet.

"Let's go."

Meghan exited the bathroom and the girls followed suit. Meghan wasn't feeling to well and decided to call a cab since, she gave the rental back. Meghan stared out the window, rubbing her achy tummy. She noticed a cab pulling up and stopped in front of their apartment.

"The cab's here. Let's go." Meghan just wanted to go to the store to buy a pregnancy test, but she knew if she tested positive, she would eventually have to go to the doctor sooner or later.

At the hospital, Meghan sat on the bed in the ER, swinging her legs back and forth, waiting for the doctor to return. She had already peed in the cup, and now she was just waiting for the results. There was a knock on the door, and after she confirmed it was the doctor, she told her to come in. She nervously bit down on her bottom lip as the doctor came into the room smiling. She held her clipboard in her arms, clutching it to her chest.

"You're pregnant."

"I am?" Meghan's eyes lit up. "How many weeks am I?"

"Based on your last menstrual period, I would say you are about eight weeks pregnant," she informed Meghan as she placed her clipboard on the table and put on some gloves. "Come with me." The doctor led Meghan to another room. "Lay down on the exam table, please."

Meghan did as she said and turned her head. When she did, the paper she laid on cackled. She watched as the doctor pulled a machine closer to her and sat on a rolling chair, pulling it next to the exam table.

"Pull up your shirt for me, please."

Meghan slowly pulled up her white tank top and tucked it underneath her bra's wiring. Meghan jumped at the touch of a cool gel being placed on her tummy.

"Sorry about that." The doctor chuckled. "I should have warned you it's a little cold."

"It's okay." Meghan smiled, propping up her head under her crossed arms as she watched the doctor rub the gel on her stomach.

"Ohhhh," the doctor cooed. "Look at what we have here."

Meghan looked up at the sonogram screen and couldn't tell what she was so excited for besides the fact that it was a baby. "What?"

"You're having twins," she said as she pointed to the screen, pointing at two separate placentas.

Meghan almost fainted when she said "twins". She gulped down hard and looked at the doctor as if she had five heads. "W-what did you say?" Meghan asked, making sure the doctor was correct the first time. When the doctor repeated herself, she knew she wasn't hard of hearing. Meghan smiled and shook her head in disbelief.

"Thanks, Doctor," Meghan said as she sighed dejectedly, lying back down. She was happy, but she just didn't know how Jamal would take the unexpected news.

She felt the doctor rubbing off the gel with a napkin before tossing it into the trash. "I will prescribe you some prenatal vitamins to take," the doctor said as she sat down at her desk and shook the mouse for the screen to come on. "You take these once a day." After the doctor wrote her prescription, she exited the room.

Meghan sat up in the bed and pulled her shirt down. She slid off the bed and slipped on her sneakers. She knew the girls were going to go crazy when she told them the news. Meghan dragged her feet as she walked out into the waiting room where Carmen and Nicolette sat. They each had their eyeballs glued to the pages of the magazine. They didn't see Meghan standing before them with her hands on her hips. Meghan rolled her eyes and cleared her throat to get their undivided attention.

"Shit!" Carmen cursed. "You scared me!" She held her chest as she sighed loudly. "So what did the doctor say?"

"I'm pregnant." Meghan smiled. "And…"

"And what?" Carmen titled her head to the side, wondering what else it could be.

"I'm having twins." Meghan shrugged her shoulders stiffly with a smile on her face.

"Get the fuck out of here!" Nicolette exclaimed as she stood up.

Meghan slowly placed down her shoulders and bobbed her head up and down. "Yup."

"Congratulations!" Carmen and Nicolette said in unison. They hugged her as Carmen rubbed her belly.

"Twins? Oh God, bless your heart!"

They all chuckled. Meghan started to walk down the corridors of the hospital with her girls in tow.

"Are you going to tell Jamal?"

"Of course I am! I mean, I have to," Meghan said. "I'm not taking care of these babies on my own. He will be in their lives too." Meghan smiled.

"What do you think he will say?" Carmen asked curiously.

"I don't know." Meghan shrugged her shoulders. "What else can he say but 'I will help you take care of our children'? He is the one who kept having sex without the condom on knowingly, so he obviously knew what he was doing."

"I'm sure he did! Hmph," Nicolette said as they pushed past the swinging doors. Once outside, she continued talking. "I bet he had that planned so he could trap your ass."

"Why would he want to trap a girl like me?"

"Why wouldn't he?" Nicolette asked. "Well, I think it may be the other way around." She twirled her finger around in the air in small circles.

"Well, excuse you!" Meghan stopped in her tracks as she stared at Nicolette. "I'm not the one who knew he didn't have a condom on. I'm not trying to trap him. He just fell in love with your girl. He never had anything like this before." Meghan winked, snapping her fingers, impersonating a down south accent as she rolled her hips like a dancer. The girls broke out into laughter as they made their way to the car.

When Meghan reached their apartment, she immediately called Jamal. He informed her that he was in the middle of something, but would be there as soon as he could. After their first rendezvous, they would go out occasionally, but lately he'd been extremely busy with work. She could only imagine how he did it. She assumed that running two businesses wasn't easy.

Meghan patiently waited for Jamal as she lay on the queen-sized bed, twirling a strand of hair, contemplating how she would tell him. She was nervous and figured he would tell her to get an abortion or something.

There was a slight knock on the front door to their apartment causing Meghan to stop twirling her hair, and quickly turned her head towards the door. Before Meghan could get out of the bed, Nicolette opened up the door wearing some skimpy clothes. Meghan rolled her eyes as she jumped out of the bed and made her way to the door.

Nicolette was still standing there as she held open the door for Jamal.

"I got it," Meghan stated with a stern voice as she closed the door. "Go put some clothes on. I have company." She eyeballed Nicolette, who playfully rolled her eyes and went to her bedroom that was next to the front door of their apartment. Meghan cleared her throat when she noticed Jamal looking at her best friend as she walked off. Meghan cleared her throat again, snapping him out of his trance.

"My fault." He cleared his throat and hugged her. "You look beautiful," he complimented her as he pulled away from the hug, eyeing her up and down.

"I guess." Meghan smiled as she shrugged her shoulders. "I just threw something on this morning. I wasn't about to get all fancy and whatnot just to go to the hospital."

"Hospital? For what?"

Meghan sat on the edge of the bed, folding up one leg underneath her thigh.

"Meghan?"

She pretended like she didn't hear his question. "Huh?"

"Why did you go to the hospital?" Jamal asked as he sat down beside her on the edge of the bed. "Is everything okay?"

"Yeah, I'm just fine." Meghan smiled as she caressed the back of her neck. "I have to tell you something…and I don't want you to be upset."

"Why would I be upset?" Jamal asked. "You can tell me anything," he assured her as he turned towards her and grabbed one of her hands and kissed it. "Anything."

She cracked a smile and stared Jamal in his eyes. "I'm pregnant, Jamal," Meghan spoke in a low tone, petrified of what his response would be.

He stood up from the bed and walked back and forth, pacing the floor.

"If you don't want to me to have this baby -"

Jamal cut her off. "Why wouldn't I?" He worked up a smile.

"So you're not mad?" Meghan asked, surprised.

"No. I've always wanted to have children," he informed her "I can't have my girl living in a little-ass apartment like this.," he said, looking around. "I mean, it's nice and everything, but this is no place suitable for you and you're pregnant too. "

"Oh, so now I'm your girl?" Meghan asked, avoiding everything else he had said after that. She was smiling from ear to ear when she heard him call her his girl. He didn't even ask her, but she figured it was fine with her.

"Well, unless you don't want to be." He winked as he sat down next to her and said, "I can't have you living here with my kid, living with two other woman. I mean no offense to your friends but that just isn't happening."

"Kids," Meghan corrected him with a smile.

"Kids?" His eyebrows arched and he had a baffled expression written on his face.

"Yes. We're having twins." Meghan's eyebrows arched up, hoping he could handle not just one, but two kids.

"That's alright; the more the merrier." They both laughed. Jamal cleared his throat and took Meghan's hand, staring at her with sincerity in his eyes. "I know you may think that I'm crazy, but I would like you to move in with me."

Meghan couldn't believe what she was hearing. She hadn't known Jamal for that long, and he was already moving faster than she was. But everything that he was saying, she wanted to hear. Meghan rose to her feet and walked towards the vanity mirror. She placed her hands on the edge of the table, looking into the mirror but staring at Jamal. She didn't want him to think that he could win her over so easily. In actuality, he already had. Meghan already had her mind made up.

Jamal got up and walked behind her, wrapping his arms around her waist. "Look, Meghan, I know we haven't known each other that long, but…I want to be a part of my children's lives," he stated as he rubbed her flat stomach. "I mean, if you don't want to move in with me, or be my girl…I will still always be in my kids' lives," Jamal said with sincerity. He removed his arms from her stomach and started to walk away. He was getting the idea that she didn't want to have any relations with him.

"Jamal!" Meghan called out, causing Jamal to stop in his tracks and turn around. "I would love to be your girl. I would love to move in with you. And I would love for you to be there for your children. They need both parents…not just one." Meghan smiled as she walked over towards him, wrapping her arms tightly around his neck. "I just didn't think you would feel the same way I feel about you, but now I know you do," Meghan whispered in his ear before pulling away from the embrace and kissing him on the lips.

"Well, start packing your stuff," Jamal said, smiling as he clapped his hands and rubbed them together.

"This is so surreal!" Meghan said to herself as she started packing the little bit of stuff she had in her luggage.

Nicolette and Carmen must have been eavesdropping the whole time because Nicolette came in there asking questions.

"Where the hell do you think your going?" Meghan looked up and chuckled nervously.

"Um, I'm moving in with Jamal," she informed them. "It was his idea."

"Yes, it was my idea…so don't be mad at her," Jamal assured the ladies. "I can't have the mother of my children living in a small apartment raising two children."

"So what about us?" Carmen asked with a stern tone, arched eyebrows, and her arms folded across her breasts. "How are we going to afford to live in this apartment by ourselves? You had extra money that helped us cover the rest of rent. "

Meghan had never seen Carmen get like that with her, but she knew she was just upset by her leaving them.

Jamal cleared his throat "I'll be downstairs in the car," Jamal said with half a smirk and his eyes widened. He had nothing to do with this, so he decided to excuse himself. He grabbed her luggage and headed out the door. Meghan walked over to the mirror, opened up her purse, and pulled out some money. Meghan didn't have much left, after paying for the hotel, shopping, and buying groceries for the month and a half. She was also on a payment plan, paying for cosmetology school for her and Carmen. Her money was dwindling down. She hoped she would find a part time job in a hair salon because she didn't want to be broke. After the rest of her money was gone, she really would be completely broke. But Meghan didn't worry too much because she knew Jamal would take care of her physically and financially.

"Take this," Meghan said as she peeled off more than ten hundred dollar bills. She handed half of the money to each of them.

"Y'all time is coming soon…I just know it is," Meghan assured them, but it didn't seem like they were buying it. "Listen, Nicolette, that guy John…he likes you…really, really likes you. And Carmen, I know Romeo just got out of a recent divorce, but he has eyes on you. Y'all will soon get what we came for. We will live the lavish life. Just keep your eyes on the prize. I love y'all." Meghan smiled with tears in her eyes as she hugged both of her best friends.

"Love you too," Nicolette said, prolonging her words.

"Love you, Meghan, I'm happy for you," Carmen admitted as she wiped away a single tear that escaped her right eye and trickled down her cheek.

"I'll call y'all later on tonight." Meghan grabbed her purse and headed out the front door. She felt weird leaving her friends like that, but she wasn't going to let her friends come between her and Jamal. She had an opportunity, and she sure enough was going to take it.

7 Months Later

Meghan

Several months ago, you couldn't even tell Meghan was pregnant. Now she was big as a balloon, carrying two twins around in her stomach. She was so lucky she was in the last month of pregnancy. She was also glad that cosmetology school was over for her. She was exhausted from the long hours she had to stand on her feet. Towards the end of school, the money she had was all gone. She didn't have any more money to pay for Cosmetology school. The first thing that came to mind was how she wasn't going to be able to pay for Carmen's tuition to. Although Carmen had a part-time job working at the MAC store, She was just worried how Carmen was going to be able to afford her intuition. And she also had to pay for the rent her and Nicolette had to now split. Carmen told her not to worry about her cost of the school, she would make a way to pay it. Meghan's worries flew out the window when Jamal found out she couldn't afford the school anymore, and paid off the rest of her cosmetology school in full.

Meghan sat in the passenger seat of her fiancé's yellow Ferrari as he sped down the streets of Palm Beach. "Slow down, Jamal," Meghan begged with her hands rubbing her protruding belly and her eyes sealed shut.

A few minutes ago, Jamal had told her to close her eyes and that he had a surprise for her. They had just come from her celebrating her greatest accomplishment yet: graduating from cosmetology school. She could feel the car coming to a complete stop. She kept fidgeting, trying hard not to sneak a peek. She could feel Jamal wrapping a blindfold across her eyes.

"I already have my eyes closed, Jamal." Meghan sighed.

"It's okay; this is just so you won't try to sneak a peek." Jamal smiled as he tied a loose knot in the back of her head.

Meghan waited patiently as Jamal got out of the car and opened up her door to help her out. Meghan took his hand and stepped out of the car slowly, holding one hand on her stomach. Her white, summery dress blew as the wind passed them. Meghan stood on the sidewalk. All she could hear was cars passing and people talking on the sidewalk.

"Are you ready?" Jamal asked as he stood behind Meghan and whispered in her ear.

"Yes, I'm ready, babe. Come on and take this blindfold off of me," she insisted. She could feel his hands as they touched the back of her head and he untied the knot. The blindfold fell freely from her eyes but she still held her eyes closed.

"You can open them."

Meghan's eyes fluttered up and down before they opened up completely. She looked up and noticed she was standing in front of a hair salon.

"Look up," Jamal urged.

Meghan looked up and read ***Palm Beach's Finest Salon*** in a lit-up flamboyant pink color, outlined in gold. Meghan covered her mouth with her hand as tears built up at a quick pace. She had her very own hair salon, thanks to her fiancé. She turned around, hugging him as she wrapped her arms around his neck.

"Thank you…thank you…thank you!" Meghan kissed him on the lips between each thank you.

Jamal wiped off the nude lip gloss that Meghan had plastered on her lips and transferred to his and smiled.

"You're welcome. Let's check it out," he said as he gestured her towards the front door.

Meghan peeked inside but it was dark, so she couldn't see anything. Once Jamal unlocked the door to the salon, the lights came on and people screamed, "SURPRISE!"

Startled, Meghan held her hand over her beating heart. Breathing heavily, she cracked a smile. Her best friends Nicolette and Carmen were there, accompanied by their boyfriends, John and Romeo along with a few other people there they had met during their stay in Palm Beach. Several tears fell from her eyes as people congratulated her, telling her how beautiful her salon was. She didn't bother wiping the tears away because they were tears of joy. Meghan looked around her salon. It contained cheetah print salon chairs, and even the carpet throughout the salon was cheetah print carpet. Gigantic curvy mirrors were situated above each and every station. Meghan looked at Jamal in disbelief, knowing he couldn't have pulled this off all by himself.

"This is beautiful, babe." Meghan smiled as she looked around the salon one more time before turning her attention back on her fiancé. "Who helped you do this?" she asked while swirling hair around her index finger.

"Well, I had Carmen and Nicolette help me a little bit, but most of it was me." He winked as Nicolette playfully smacked his shoulder.

"Yeah, we helped out a lot, if you ask me." She smiled.

"Well, thank you all. This hair salon is so beautiful," Meghan boasted. "But…I don't even have any clientele."

"Don't worry about it; the clients will come," Jamal assured her. "I'll be back, babe." He kissed Meghan on the cheek. "Excuse me, ladies and gents." Jamal stuck his hands in his slacks and walked off, greeting the other guests.

"Of course they will!" Carmen added in. "You're the best hair stylist I know. As soon as they get their hair done once here, trust me, they will be back." Carmen said, reassuring her as she bobbed her head up in down.

"Aww, thanks." Meghan smiled as she rubbed her friend on the shoulder, thanking her. As soon as Meghan started to walk off to see the rest of her salon, she felt a sharp, painful contraction shoot through her body.

"Argh!" Meghan bent over and squeezed her eyes together as she held her stomach. Meghan forced herself not to cry. The pain that she was experiencing was something she never felt before. She clenched her jaws tightly together, making her teeth clamp down hard like a lion's would do to its prey.

"Are you okay, Meghan?" Carmen asked as she placed her hand on her friend's back.

Meghan unclenched her jaw and spoke slowly. "Yeah, I'm okay," Meghan moaned as she stood up and started to walk over to the back of the salon where the hair dryers were set up. A sharp contraction was brimming in her stomach, causing her to stop in her tracks. As soon as she did, Meghan felt a warm trickle down both sides of her legs, which were now trembling. She almost thought she had peed herself, but she remembered the doctor informing her that it would most likely be her water breaking if she felt like that. Her girls ran to her aide.

"Do you think you're having the baby? Nicolette asked as she noticed Meghan just standing there in shock.

The contraction was so tight, she couldn't even talk. She just pointed down to the floor where her water had just broken.

"Ohhh, shoot, she's having her baby!" Carmen mustered. "Jamal, she's having her baby!" she shouted out loud this time so Jamal could come over.

The girls helped her sit down on the cheetah print couch that was right behind where Meghan stood.

"Ohhh…" Meghan formed her lips into an "O" shape, trying to breathe in and out as her doctor had instructed her to do. She rubbed her belly as if it would help ease the contractions. Jamal rushed over to her side and bent down and got on his knees.

"You need me to call the doctor?" Jamal asked with a baffled expression on is face.

"Take me to the hospital." Meghan's eyes got wide as she spoke through gritted teeth.

"Okay…okay." Jamal panicked as he stood up, pacing back and forth. Jamal was distraught when he saw his wife in pain, blocking him from doing what he was supposed to.

"JAMAL!" Meghan shrieked as another contraction shot through her stomach.

"Take me to the hospital!" She spoke so quickly it made Jamal's head spin.

Jamal quickly helped Meghan get to her feet. She didn't even want to walk. It hurt too much and all she could think of was how strong the contractions were. With each step, she felt like they were worse. She just wanted to stop and sit down, but Jamal kept forcing her to the car. Jamal opened up the passenger side door and helped Meghan carefully into the car. Once inside, Jamal rushed around the hood of the car and hopped into the driver's side. He turned on the car, placed the car in drive, and peeled off, leaving tread marks on the street. He was speeding to the hospital as if he was Batman in his Batmobile. He just really hoped that he didn't get pulled over with the way he was speeding.

Jamal's mouth was open as he looked over at his fiancée. He couldn't fathom the amount of pain she was enduring. However, he could see the pain in her face and the way she was holding onto the door handle for dear life. Meghan started to contract every three minutes. She knew she was in labor. With every minute the contractions became very intense and painful. She didn't know what to do so she held onto the door and bit down hard, grinding her teeth together. It still didn't help with the contractions. She tried to get her mind off of it, but she couldn't.

As soon as he arrived at the hospital, he got out of the car quickly and ran into the hospital. He didn't bother asking for help. He grabbed an abandoned wheelchair and wheeled it out swiftly. He opened up the door for his wife and helped her get out and into the wheelchair. He wheeled her inside the hospital and informed the front desk that her water had broken and she was having her babies. Meghan sat in the chair as a strong, unbearable contraction came on. She held her head down, squeezing both of her hands into tight balls.

The receptionist paged a nurse from the back, and within seconds, one came running out. Meghan was rushed into the labor and delivery room where she would give birth to the twins. Meghan begged the doctors to give her the epidural, but it was too late. She was already eight centimeters dilated.

Jamal was right by her side with each and every push as he clutched her hand. Meghan squeezed his hand, causing him to make amusing faces.

"Damn, I didn't know she was that damn strong!" Jamal mustered through gritted teeth.

"Ohhh…I feel a contraction!" Meghan moaned.

"PUSH!" Jamal encouraged her as she gritted her teeth together and mustered out a loud grunt, pushing until she couldn't push anymore.

Her long, thick hair was now starting to curl up as she began to sweat. Beads of sweat began to decorate her forehead and she was now sweating profusely.

"PUSH!" Jamal said again.

She squeezed his hand with all of her potential as she took a deep breath and pushed with all of the strength she had left. Meghan's scream was lingering as she felt the head and then the rest of the body of one of her babies come out. Piercing cries escaped the baby's mouth, letting her know her baby was alive. Meghan blinked her eyes several times as she cried. She thought it was over, almost forgetting she had one more baby to push out. Meghan pushed so hard that the next twin came out within seconds of delivering the first. The second baby cried as well. Meghan thanked God. Slowly, she let go off Jamal's hand as she sighed in relief. She looked up at the ceiling, blinking away the tears that submerged her eyes. She was so happy the contractions and the pushing were over.

With a bowed head, she took a moment to thank God for a safe delivery. Jamal fixed the hospital bed, accommodating it so she could sit up.

"You did it." Jamal smiled as he rubbed the sweat from Meghan's forehead. "I didn't know you were that strong, or I wouldn't have gave you my hand." He smiled.

Meghan playfully smacked him on the shoulder, as her eyes wandered across the room. The doctor was weighing her twin baby girls, getting them ready. A smile appeared on her face and tears trickled down both sides of her cheeks as she watched her babies being brought over to her. The doctor placed both babies in her arms, one on the right, one to the left. Meghan cherished this moment in her heart, vowing to never forget it. Her daughters were beautiful. They were identical; you could hardly tell them apart. The only thing that distinguished the two from each other was that one of them had a tiny beauty mark on the side of her eye.

"Her name is going to be Kimberley," Meghan smiled, referring to the baby with the beauty mark. "And Kim." Meghan smiled as she caressed Kim's cheek with her index finger. Her daughters were light-skinned with slanted eyes that made them appear to be Asian, a head fully of curly hair, and small lips. Meghan reminisced on her baby pictures, and they shared a resemblance.

"Can I hold one of my babies?" Jamal asked with his hands out.

Meghan smiled, gesturing with one of her arms to Kim, who was closest to him.

***

After Meghan had her twin babies, a month flew by quickly. She was already standing in front of her soon-to-be husband as they exchanged vows. Meghan looked beautiful with a white veil covering her face. Her hair was tamed nicely into an updo hairstyle with her hair swooped in the front over her eye. Expensive, gleaming diamonds adorned her neck, ears, and arms. Although Meghan had only recently come to Palm Beach and barely knew anyone, her wedding was packed with people who she knew, friends of Jamal's, and friends of friends. Meghan was happy that her mother-in-law Evelyn was there at her wedding.

Meghan wished her mother Loretta could've come. It made her sad that her own mother didn't attend her wedding. She had called her days before the wedding informing her that she had two beautiful twin girls and that she had a wedding she would like her mother to attend, but she declined. She hadn't talked to her mother since she left Boston. She tried talking to her, but her mother would just ignore her phone calls.

Meghan pushed her mother out of her mind. She stared at her husband as he spoke.

"I, Jamal, take you, Meghan, to be my beloved wife, to have and to hold you, to honor you, to treasure you, to be at your side in sorrow and in joy, in the good times and in the bad, and to love and cherish you always. I promise you this from my heart, for all the days of my life." After they exchanged vows, he slid the ring on her finger and they kissed passionately.

Meghan cried. She didn't want to mess up her make up, but she couldn't help it. She had come a long way since she first moved to Palm Beach. She really didn't think she would meet a wealthy man, get pregnant, have twins, and get married within the same year. They were tears of joy, and she didn't stop them from falling.

As they walked down the aisle together hand in hand, she basked in the moment. Everyone was clapping, smiling for them, and congratulating them as they exited out of the church. Their twin girls waited for them in two white custom-made carriages.

Meghan grabbed Kimberley and Jamal grabbed Kim. Meghan stared into Jamal's eyes and smiled.

"For better or worse."

"For better or worse," Jamal said as he leaned in and kissed her on the forehead.

Nicolette

Nicolette felt as if it was just yesterday she had moved to Palm Beach. She had to admit she was living the good life. Nicolette was thankful and she felt like John had been placed in her life for a reason. Several weeks after she started working at his mother's boutique, he told her she could stay with him and his mother. At first she declined. She didn't want Carmen to live by herself in the apartment. She knew that she wouldn't be able to afford fifteen hundred dollars all by herself. The money Nicolette earned from the boutique was helping towards their rent

Reluctantly, Carmen decided it was best for Nicolette to move in with John. She didn't want to be a burden in Nicolette's life if she turned him down. She figured her day would soon come. She hoped that Romeo would make the same moves as his friends did.

At first Nicolette was staying in John's oversized guest room, which had its own bathroom and balcony. In a way she was offended, but she realized he was really trying to help her out. A job, a place to stay…he had even bought her a white Range Rover just to get back and forth to his mother's boutique. Nicolette couldn't thank him enough. Within the last month of her staying with him, John had asked if they could take their relationship to another level. She moved out of the guest room into John's master bedroom. Nicolette automatically assumed he would propose to her since her best friend Meghan was already married. She got way ahead of herself. He only had asked her to be his girlfriend, but she gladly accepted.

Nicolette stood at the counter of the boutique as she wrapped up a long box and placed a red bow on top of it for a customer. She smiled as she placed the box in a big bag and thanked her for shopping at Lily's Boutique. A loud thump startled Nicolette and she looked around the store to see if anything had fallen. She then remembered Lily telling her she was going to the bathroom about ten minutes ago, and she had never come back out.

"Lily!" Nicolette called out as she ran around the counter and into the back room. She tried to open the door, but it was locked. She twisted and turned the knob, trying to pry the door open, and she knew that it wasn't going to work.

Nicolette knew that John's mother was on painkillers and she was hoping she hadn't taken too many. Just the other day Lily had taken one too many pills because she forgot whether she had taken them or not. Nicolette remembered that Lily had a set of keys that unlocked the bathroom door from the outside. She emerged from the back room and snatched the keys from behind the counter. As she made her way back, she fell on the floor and dropped the keys. She got up and rushed to the bathroom door, searching for the key. It took her several tries before finding the right key to open up the door.

Nicolette nearly fainted when she saw Miss Lily lying on the floor she appeared to be asleep. A container of open pills was lying sitting on top of the sink. Nicolette dropped to her knees and checked to see if she had a pulse and she did.

"You're going to be alright, Miss Lily," Nicolette informed her as she removed her cell phone from her purse and dialed 911.

The dispatcher was asking so many questions that she felt like hanging up, but she didn't. She told her the address and the dispatcher informed her that the ambulance was on its way. Several minutes passed by and the ambulance finally arrived. They were taking Lily out on a stretcher, placing her into an ambulance. Quickly, Nicolette locked up the shop since she and Lily were the only two who worked there. She hopped in the ambulance as it hauled them away.

Nicolette had been so busy focusing on Lily that she had forgotten to call John and tell him what happened. She texted John, informing him that his mother had overdosed on her medicine and that they were heading to Palm Beach Gardens Medical Center. It was the closet hospital to the boutique.

After arriving at the hospital, Nicolette made sure she stood by Lily's side the entire time. The doctor informed her she couldn't stay in the room and had to wait in the waiting room. Nicolette waited in the waiting room as the doctors tried to resuscitate her. Several minutes later, the doctor emerged from the back and walked over to Nicolette who rose to her feet. She apologized to her and walked into the back. Tears brimmed in her eyes as she followed behind the doctor. Her feet dragged as she walked into the room and over to Lily. She broke down crying. She couldn't believe she was dead. She had gotten so close to her since the first day she started working for her.

She sat by her side and held onto her hand, staring at her. She knew that once John got the news of his mother's death, he would be devastated. Fifteen minutes passed by and in walked John.

"How is she?"

Nicolette automatically knew that he hadn't been informed that his mother had died. She didn't want to be the one to break it to him, but she had no choice. Nicolette jumped to her feet and rushed over to John and embraced him tightly.

"I'm so sorry, John." She rubbed his back, squeezing him tightly.

"Sorry what?" He pushed away from the embrace and rushed over to his mother. She appeared to be sleeping, but in actuality, she was dead.

"She's dead, John," Nicolette said in a low tone. "She took too many pills."

John busted out into a hysterical cry as he dropped to his knees. She had never seen him cry like this before. Actually, she had never even seen him cry at all. She walked over to him and he hugged her while sitting on the floor with his face buried in her stomach. She rubbed his smooth bald head as tears escaped her eyes. She felt like she had just lost her mother all over again.

***

Dressed in all black, Nicolette and John walked hand in hand down the aisle of the funeral home. Nicolette nodded her head at Meghan. She was sitting in the back with her husband as they each held one of the twins as they slept. Carmen and Romeo sat alongside of them, holding hands.

They walked up to the all-white customized casket with luxurious onyx velvet interior trim. Nicolette's eyes filled with tears as she stared down at Lily. Although she was deceased, she was beautiful. Her gray hair was curled loosely and there was a light pink lipstick color on her lips. She wore a beautiful dress that Lily had customized herself. Several authentic strands of pearls draped her neck and she was wearing the matching pearl earrings. She definitely went out in style.

John broke down at the casket when he saw his mother. Nicolette rubbed his back as he leaned forward with both hands holding the side of the casket. She knew that he needed her more than ever now. Although he didn't know her mother, there were plenty of nights she stayed up crying, wishing her mother was still alive, and John was there, comforting her in every way that he could. Even when he was at work, if she called him crying, he would come home every chance he could to be there with her. So therefore, she would be with John now every step of the way. She felt like she owed that to him.

After the funeral was over, they headed back to the house. Nicolette was upstairs sitting on the master bed, kicking off her high heels. She rubbed her feet, sighing dejectedly as she removed her clip from her hair, letting her long hair fall freely. She threw her head forward and back and ran her hand through her hair, massaging it. A smile appeared on her face when she noticed John leaning against the doorframe.

"What's up, honey? You okay?" Nicolette asked as she slipped out of her dress and tossed it to the bed. She stood there in nothing but the silk gown that hugged her slim body, accentuating the small waist Nicolette worked hard for.

"Yeah, I'm fine." John sighed as he slowly walked in the room with his hands folded across his chest. "I miss her so much, you know."

"I know," she whispered softly, wrapping her arms around his neck. "I know what it's like to lose a mother, but now it's like I lost another mother." A single tear escaped her eye. "Your mother was a beautiful person with a great heart," she reminded him.

"Yeah, you are right." He smiled, bobbing his head. "I know we shouldn't be discussing this now, but I would like you to run my mother's boutique."

"No…"

"Yes; it's yours," he informed her. "You're the only one she would want to take over it. She showed you how to design dresses and everything. You're the perfect candidate." He winked. "And plus, there's no way I'm running that boutique."

Without another word, she hugged him tightly, thanking him. "I will make your mother proud."

"I know you will." Nicolette pulled away from the embrace and he took both of her hands. "She also wanted me to give you this." He let go of her hands and placed it in his back pocket, revealing a black box.

"That's not what I think it is…is it?" Her eyebrows arched up.

"Will you marry me?" He got on one knee, opening up the box, holding it up.

"Honey, I don't want you to marry me just because your mother - "

"No, that's not it. I knew once we connected that I would make you my wife. I just didn't want to rush into anything in the beginning. I gave you your space. I didn't want you to think I was rushing anything." John wiped a tear from his left eye. "I can't see myself without you, Nicolette. I love you."

"I love you too, John Porter."

"Will you be Mrs. Porter?"

"YES!" Nicolette smiled. "Of course I will marry you, Mr. Porter."

John slid the beautiful diamond ring on her finger, which sparkled from every angle. After he slid the ring on her finger, she wrapped her arms around his neck and kissed him passionately. After she was done kissing him, she stood there for several seconds eyeing her gorgeous ring. She couldn't believe John had proposed to her.

"Hello, Mrs. Porter," she cooed with a smile as she extended her hand out, wiggling her hand. She couldn't wait to tell the girls the news.

Carmen

Carmen remembered as if it was yesterday. She was sleeping with the landlord in exchange for the cost of the rent. After Meghan and Nicolette left, she couldn't afford to pay fifteen hundred dollars for rent all by herself. So she had no choice but to put her body to use and pay for the rent with her body. She'd also been working in the mall at the MAC store as a beauty consultant for several months. She didn't make that much money, but she loved doing what she did. When Meghan's money dwindled down, Carmen had to pick up some extra shifts to help pay for her school. After she graduated cosmetology school alongside of Meghan, she decided it was time to put her talent out there for people to see. She even got side jobs going to people's houses to do their makeup for special occasions. Now she worked both part-time in Nicolette's boutique and at the MAC store.

With the money she had saved up over the past months, she had rented a studio apartment. Romeo had introduced her to one of his real estate friends who had a studio apartment that rented for about $900 a month, all utilities included. She was lucky. She felt hugely relieved when she signed her lease. She hated sleeping with the landlord just so that she could stay in a three-bedroom apartment, something she clearly didn't need. Plenty of times Meghan and Carmen invited her into her their homes until she could get on her feet, but she declined and told them she was okay, that she could pay for it, and they believed her.

Popping her strawberry bubblegum, Carmen pulled a small pocket mirror out of her purse. She turned her head from side to side as she pushed up her hair, which was curled tightly. She grabbed a lipstick from her purse, gliding the lipstick back and forth on her plump lips, making sure she did it perfectly. Carmen was obsessed when it came down to makeup and she always made sure her face was beautifully decorated.

"You're supposed to be working, not trying to look cute." Nicolette playfully rolled her eyes as she emerged from the back carrying a box that held a new shipment for the store.

"Yeah, well, Romeo is supposed to be stopping by," Carmen informed her, taking one last look before closing the mirror. "I have to make sure I look fabulous." Carmen gave Nicolette a quick smile.

"Don't worry; you look fine," Nicolette assured her. "Just know that looking fine doesn't pay the bills."

Oh yes it can, Carmen thought to herself. She knew that looks could damn near pay for anything, depending on the person you were dealing with.

"Here, unpack these dresses and hang them up," Nicolette said politely as she slid the big box onto the counter. She took a razor and slit it in the middle, cutting the tape instantly. She opened up the box and started unpacking the plastic paper the dresses came packed in.

Carmen was looking at the beautiful dresses and she smiled. One of them she picked up was a wedding dress. On the low, Carmen was jealous that Meghan was married and Nicolette was getting married. She knew that she and Romeo liked each other, but she also knew he wasn't ready to be in a marriage again.

The front door chimed, indicating someone had walked into the boutique. Carmen looked up from what she was doing and noticed Romeo walking in. Her panties got wet within seconds of seeing him. He was wearing a tight white shirt, showing off his athletic body. He wore all-black jeans and a white and gold Gucci belt with all-white sneakers. His dark hair was curly and silky and he looked as if he just had gotten out of a shower. He looked very plain, but the gold diamond ring he wore on his pinky and gold Rolex that adorned his wrist accentuated his looks.

Although Carmen and Romeo had known each other for a little over ten months, they had only been officially dating for a couple of months. They weren't as close as Meghan and Nicolette were with their men. Carmen was a tad bit jealous, but she knew in due time he would eventually make it serious. He was extremely busy showing houses all the time and running around doing his own thing and Carmen was so busy with her own life that they didn't see each other like that. All she wanted was to spend more time with him.

"Hi, baby." Romeo walked over to the counter. Simultaneously, they both leaned forward and gave each other a kiss on the cheek. Carmen would rather kiss him on the lips since his face was so stubbly, but due to having on lipstick, she couldn't. "You look absolutely beautiful," he complimented her.

"Thanks." Carmen blushed as she looked at him and examined his face. "You got some lipstick on your cheek." Carmen giggled. "Let me get that for you," she insisted as she licked the back of her thumb and wiped the lipstick off his face, not wanting to scratch his sexy face with her long, French-manicured nails.

"These are for you." He handed her a bouquet of fresh roses.

Carmen hadn't even noticed that he had them in his hand when he entered the boutique. She was too busy admiring how handsome he was.

"Aww, que lindo!" Carmen sniffed the roses and the aroma tickled her sensitive nose, causing her to sneeze. She quickly put them down on the counter.

"God bless you, beautiful."

"Thank you, Romeo." She covered her nose as she sneezed again. "These are so beautiful, Romeo, thank you."

"You're welcome. I was going to see if you were free so we could grab a bite to eat."

"Umm…well, I'm working right now, and - "

"Go on, Carmen." Nicolette appeared from the back, smiling, as if she had been eavesdropping the entire time. "It's not that busy today, so you can go on." She winked at her and walked behind the desk. “I can finish from here.” She was referring to the new shipment.

“Thanks, Nicolette, you are the best.” Carmen hugged her, grabbed her purse from the counter, and slid it on her arm, bringing it up to her shoulder.

“Make sure you bring her back in one piece, you hear?” Nicolette said sarcastically.

“You don’t have to worry about that,” Romeo assured her. “If anything, I would bring her back better than she left.” Romeo winked at Carmen as he took her hand and headed out of the boutique.

“I’ll see you tomorrow.”

Without turning back, Carmen waved her hand in the air. Her gold bangles jiggled, creating music. She hopped into Romeo’s Rolls Royce and he began to drive away. She placed her hand on his hand, smiling as she gawked at him. She loved the time that she got to spend with him and cherished it.

“I’ve been thinking,” Romeo said, breaking the silence as he drove with one hand on the steering wheel and the other massaging the tip of his chin.

“Been thinking about what, baby?”

“I know we haven’t been spending that much time with each other. I’m busy working, and you’re working two jobs now. I don’t want to make that an excuse as to why we can’t see each other like we should. You’re my girl now and I want to make it official.”

“Official how?” Carmen was curious to know. She was patiently waiting for him to make the move. Hell, Meghan was married with two kids and Nicolette had just gotten proposed to. She was the only one who still had the girlfriend status.

“You will see,” he smiled. “I have a surprise for you, but you have to close your eyes.”

“Okay.” Carmen closed her eyes.

Romeo pulled up to his destination and got out, rushing around the hood of the car to open the door for Carmen. He helped her out of the car and guided her up several stairs. She could hear a door opening up. She didn't know what to expect and she definitely was in for a surprise.

"Open your eyes." Carmen opened her eyes and looked around. She was standing in a brand new house. "What's this?"

"What's this?" he mocked her, trying to be funny. "This is our house."

"Our house?" She smiled from ear to ear as she walked into the kitchen first. "I like the sound of that!"

The gourmet kitchen was well designed. Granite countertops filled every inch of the kitchen. There was a stainless steel refrigerator and an oversized square table with a granite countertop and four chairs. Carmen adored the generous prep island that was built into the kitchen, where she could make her daily meals and dinners. Carmen loved this kitchen to death. She was always in the kitchen, and now she could really get comfortable with cooking in her new kitchen.

Romeo snuck up behind her and kissed her on the neck. "I see you love the gourmet kitchen. I knew you would." He spun her around and picked her up, placing his arms underneath her butt to hold her up. He then placed her down on the kitchen counter and started kissing all over her, and she knew where he was going with this.

"Mmm…mmm…" she moaned. "Not on my new gourmet granite countertops, honey." She shook her head with pursed lips.

Romeo cocked back his head with a smirk. He was mad. He thought he was about to get some in his new kitchen. He figured that he deserved it.

"Finish showing me around the house and then maybe…we can make love in our new kitchen." She winked as she walked out of the kitchen with her heels clicking across the shiny floors.

Romeo gave her a tour as if she was one of his clients. Carmen loved the way he talked about the detailing in each and every room. She loved it. There were four bedrooms and four bathrooms. She didn't know why in the world he would buy a house with all this space when it was only the two of them.

They descended a short set of stairs and Carmen headed into the living room, staring at the beautiful fireplace. Romeo emerged from the kitchen holding two glasses and a bottle of Rosé in his other hand. Carmen sat on the floor and watched as he poured her a glass of Rosé. He handed her the drink as they sat in front of the fireplace.

"This house is beautiful, babe." She caressed the side of his stubbly face.

"Not as beautiful as you," he complimented her.

She playfully nudged him with her shoulder as she stared into the fire.

"I would have never thought we would be here right now."

"It takes time for everything, Carmen," he informed her. "I'm a take my time kind of guy. Yes, I'm in love with you, but I don't like to rush things. That's how things get screwed up."

"You're right." Carmen bobbed her head, agreeing to everything he was saying as she took a small sip of her drink.

A loud knock on the door startled them both. Romeo placed his drink down beside him and jumped to his feet. He looked down at Carmen and said "Stay here. Let me see who this is." He walked over to the front door, holding it slightly ajar.

"What do you want?" Romeo demanded.

"I want you to go find her!" a woman shrieked.

Carmen stood up, walking over to see Romeo and his ex-wife with her hands folded across her breasts. She wondered what all the commotion was.

She cleared her throat. "Is there a problem, honey?" Carmen stood beside Romeo, pulling the door open so she could see his ex-wife face to face.

"No, there's not. Just go back inside."

"Oh, so this is why you return none of my phone calls, or the detective's phone calls?" Marcella pointed towards Carmen and shook her head. "You don't have to worry about me or finding your daughter, but mark my words…you will pay!" she shrieked with her finger pointed in Romeo's face before she stormed out.

Carmen watched as Marcella left mad as hell She hopped into her Mercedes Benz and peeled off, leaving tread marks on their fresh pavement.

Carmen mustered up a few words, but Romeo stopped her with his hand. He headed back into the house and she followed suit.

"What the hell is she talking about?" Carmen closed the door behind her and locked it without taking her eyes off of him. "Your daughter? When was you going to tell me you had a daughter?" She still got no answer. "Un-fucking-believable!" she barked as she started to run up the stairs.

Romeo grabbed her arm, stopping her dead in her tracks. "I'm sorry I didn't tell you," he informed her, pulling her closer to him.

"So be honest with me: what happened to your daughter?"

"She was kidnapped from the house when we lived in West Palm Beach." He walked into the kitchen, leaning against the table with his palms pressed against the counter.

"I'm so sorry." Carmen rubbed his back. "Do you know who took her?"

"No, I don't. The cops think she's dead. Marcella just wants me to feel the same way she feels. I always loved my daughter and still love her until this day. I just don't know what to do. She's gone and I can't bring her back!" Romeo cried.

Carmen didn't know what to do but hold him. She seriously hoped that his ex-wife wasn't going to be a problem, but she predicted that she would be. She just hoped that she was making the right decision by being with Romeo. She didn't want to go through whatever his ex-wife was going through.

Afterword

Meghan enjoyed her life with her husband Jamal and their beautiful twin daughters Kimberley and Kim. She was a hard-working mother. She had enrolled her daughters in the best daycare in Palm Beach, making sure they were in good hands. At first she was overprotective of her children, not wanting anyone to watch them. But she had no choice since she had a business to run: her salon. Jamal was running his car lot and his insurance company, so he had his hands full. As much as he would have loved to watch his kids, he just couldn't. They were bringing in a huge amount of money from their businesses.

Although Meghan's daughters were only a couple of months old, she had already set up a college fund account for each of them. Her business was doing extremely well and she quickly became known as the best hair stylist in Palm Beach. She even put a few hair salons out of business in the area. Meghan had no worries. She was enjoying the life she lived and she cherished every moment. Not once did she regret leaving Boston.

Nicolette redecorated Lily's Boutique and also changed its name to Nikki's Boutique. At first she didn't want to change the name, but it was time for a facelift. She took the skills that Miss Lily had taught her and put them to good use. She was designing clothes for the richest women in Palm Beach, including a few select celebrities. Miss Lily was a well-known person and she brought a decent amount of clientele into the shop, but Nicolette had people flowing in and out of her boutique on the daily. While her husband was busy being a cop, protecting their city, she was being the best wife she could. She cooked him breakfast and prepared him lunch, bringing it to his job every day, and she cooked dinner every night even when he worked late. She did her duties as a wife and loved it. Her husband rewarded her with the finer things. Anything she wanted, she had gotten. Every day Nicolette hit the streets dressed lavishly, looking as if she was born rich.

Carmen and Romeo became more serious after they moved in with each other. Although he was busy showing clients properties, Carmen was glad that she now saw him every day. His ex-wife Marcella had moved away and hadn't been seen since the last day she had showed up at their house. Carmen thanked God she was gone because she didn't need another woman coming in between hers and Romeo's fresh relationship. She loved the way Romeo catered to her as if she was a queen. In her eyes, she was the queen of the castle they lived in.

Carmen was eagerly awaiting the day when Romeo would propose to her. Some days when he would surprise her, she figured he would pull out a ring, but he didn't. Carmen figured she'd just play her part for now, holding down the fort while he brought in the money. She had her little side jobs doing people's makeup, but she knew that wouldn't get her far in life. Discreetly she was working on building her own makeup line, hoping one day to see it in full effect. She desperately wanted to be a Palm Beach wife, but she would just have to wait her turn.

The girls lived the perfect life, the lives they had always dreamt of. The girls enjoyed meeting the loves of their lives. They were attending royal parties and hosting events. Meghan enjoyed being a Palm Beach wife and a mother. Nicolette couldn't wait until she married her love, John Porter. Carmen anticipated the day Romeo would propose to her, hoping to become a Palm Beach wife herself.

Little did they know that this was just the beginning…

Palm Beach Wives: The Beginning

COMING SOON!

Scarlet
RED
PINKY DIOR

PINKY DIOR

COMING SOON!

COMING SOON!

COMING SOON!

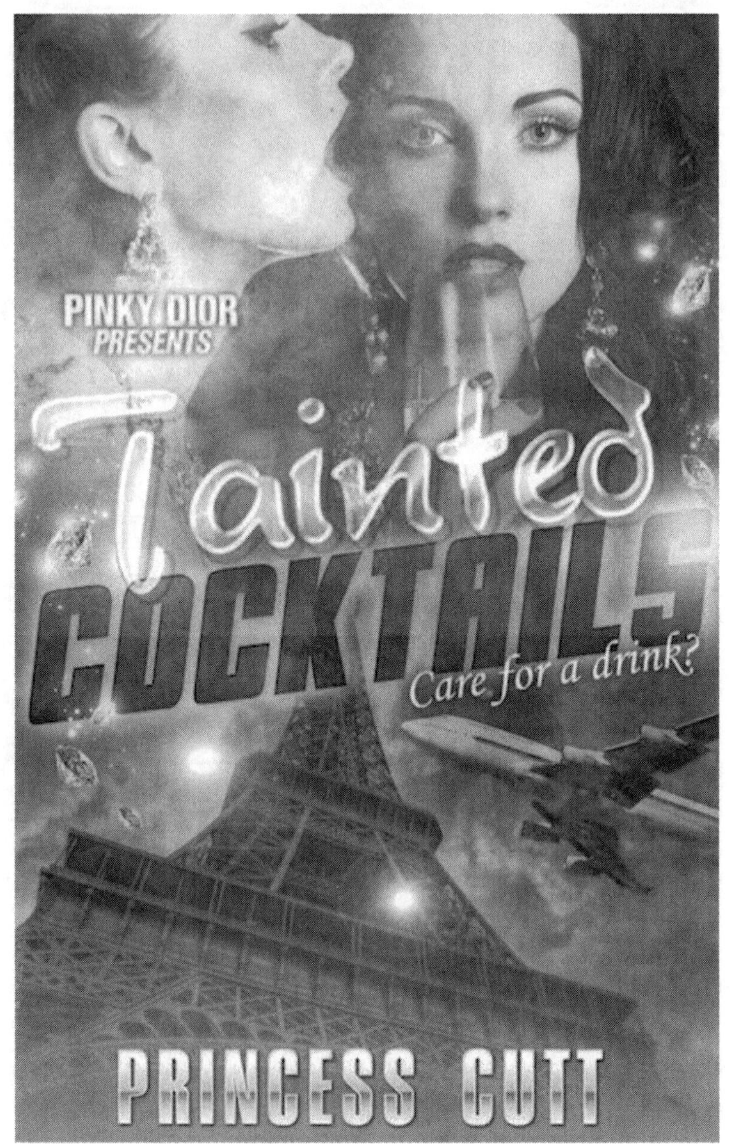

PINKY DIOR PRESENTS!

TITLES BY ME:

HAZEL EYES

HAZEL EYES 2

VALENTINES DAY MASSACRE

THE DIAMOND EXCHANGE

THE DIAMOND EXCHANGE 2

ALMIGHTY DOLLA ANTHOLOGY

BITCHES AIN'T LOYAL

PINK LIPSTICK & PISTOLS 1

PINK LIPSTICK & PISTOLS 2

THE HUSTLERS DAUGHTER

MOB DAUGHTERS

CPSIA information can be obtained at www.ICGtesting.com
Printed in the USA
LVOW07s2116201016

509597LV00013B/1076/P